THE CHOSEN OF GAIA

THE
CHOSEN OF
GAIA

M. MARIZ

© 2012 **The Chosen of Gaia** by **M. Mariz**

All rights reserved.

For my family and friends,

for making me a believer.

ONE

Sunday. The warm weather combined with the soft breeze of the early morning seemed to be holding the promise of some new and exciting adventure.

This was definitely the time for a change – a wave of boldness filled Albert's lungs.

He was fifteen now, an age when things could finally start happening, if he could rise to the challenge.

Maybe he just needed to rely more on Ruth and ask for a "social intervention". For the last couple of days they had been renting the beach house, his twin sister had learned kite surfing, won a hiking competition and even took to the sky in her first paragliding flight.

There she was on the ocean... swimming with her new friends... while he was sitting pathetically on the sand, wearing too much sunscreen, and holding an old book that he wasn't even that interested in reading.

"Albert?" a soft voice interrupted his thoughts. The kindest voice he had ever known belonged to the sweetest person he could imagine – his mom, Sarah. "I've called your name more than five times already, but you didn't even blink. Is everything okay?" Her bright green eyes were fixed on him, trying to decipher his thoughts.

"Yeah, I was just thinking about... this book. It's very interesting..." he feigned.

He knew he couldn't hide much from her, but there were a few things that he just preferred to keep to himself.

"I brought your lunch!" offered Sarah, handing him a plate with some chips and a hamburger.

"Uh-oh... Do you think Dad made it right this time?"

Hesitantly he grabbed the burger, while his mom sat next to him.

"Well... it's better than the last time..." she said, glancing at Albert's dad, Victor Klein, grilling in front of the house. Although clouds of dark smoke poured out of his makeshift grill, he seemed confident in his own performance. "Isn't your dad the best?"

"He definitely should be prohibited from any kind of food preparation," said Albert, his eyes frozen on his plate. His dad didn't use to dedicate too much of his time to family events like these, so he would try to show a little support and appreciation. After a deep breath, he gathered the courage to take his first bite. Although his gag reflex was almost instantaneous, he had to disguise his difficulty in chewing and swallowing it, after noticing his dad's glance. Albert gave him a quick thumbs up, and Victor smiled back, proudly.

"Soap seems to love it!" Sarah pointed to their basset hound, happily devouring a cooked patty that Victor had inadvertently dropped on the floor.

"Soap?" repeated Albert, discreetly spitting the food in a napkin. "He eats Ruth's makeup and even my dirty socks! He doesn't count!"

Sarah couldn't hold back a smile; Albert definitely had a point. That same week she had already caught the dog eating lemons, red peppers and her toothbrush.

"Wait—what's going on...?" Albert gasped, staring at the ocean.

The water seemed to rush away from the shoreline, as if sucked down a bath tub drain.

"Oh my God, Mom..." Albert stammered. "It's a tsunami!"

A warning siren sounded. Life guards blew their whistles and yelled evacuation orders. Surfers started to swim back desperately. Parents ran looking for their children and children started to cry. Total chaos.

Sarah grabbed held Albert's hands, in shock.

"Come on, we've got to get out of here!" instructed Albert, helping his mother to rise.

Albert scanned the horizon for Ruth. She was standing still, frozen, as if hypnotized by the retracting water.

"Ruth!" screamed Sarah.

"I'll help her, Mom, go stay with Dad!" Albert instructed.

But it wasn't easy struggling past the flow of people fleeing the beach. Like a terrified herd, they stampeded over everything and everyone in their path. His body seemed to be dragged by the others and a few times he ended up thrown on the sand along with crushed coolers and chairs.

When he finally got a hold of Ruth he knew it was too late. A colossal wave, perhaps thirty feet high, was roaring towards them. If they tried to run they would only make it a few steps. So he just stayed there, with one arm around her. His sprinting parents arrived just in time to join their embrace, and they huddled together, waiting for the water to wash everything away.

But it didn't happen. The beach houses and palm trees were knocked down. All the people and their possessions left on the beach were washed away. But not them. When the tide had settled and the Klein family reopened their eyes, they found themselves completely alone on the sand. Alone, except for a gray-haired black man, just a few steps in front of them.

He approached and looked them each in the eye, one by one. Then he announced in a deep voice:

"You have been chosen."

Albert woke up. His red hair was damp with sweat that had

trickled onto his forehead. Trying to control his quick breathing, he looked at the alarm clock on a very organized nightstand: 5:30am.

It was so insanely real, so rich with details and emotions, even his thoughts in the dream were so… genuine.

As Albert got up and his feet reached for the floor, a dog's sharp cry broke the absolute silence of the room.

"Sorry Soap!" whispered Albert, immediately caressing the dog, as an apology for squashing him.

"Quiet!" complained Ruth, sleeping across the hall… through their open doors he could make out the pile of clothes, cosmetics, purses and books on the floor around her bed. How could she live like that? He wondered.

He stumbled out towards the balcony followed faithfully by Soap.

The sun was beginning to rise, and the sky had that typical pale blue early morning color. Albert grabbed the old beach chair that was leaning against the iron bars, opened it and sat, taking a deep and reassuring breath.

"Another weird dream… that makes five now," he thought, caressing Soap's ears. Was the unconscious side of his brain trying to send some weird message with that dream, he wondered? Or was his conscious side just simplifying something that he already knew: life sucks.

Albert glanced at the sky, then sat up, startled, and rose from the chair.

The pale blue had been completely overwhelmed by reds. He rubbed his eyes. Still red! He stepped back, one foot and then another, but failed to notice Soap was once again in his way. He lost balance, and while he fell his arms smacked loudly against everything around him. Ruth woke up immediately and screamed. Soap barked instinctively.

For a few seconds Albert remained lying on the floor, with half of his body inside the bedroom, half in the balcony.

"Soap, come on! You have to stop following me like that..." complained Albert, as the dog licked his face.

His parents wondered into his doorway, looking tired and disoriented. Victor, his black hair stuck up in a faux-hawk, clutched a tennis racket defensively. Suddenly, an alarm went off and Victor spun around, swinging the racket in the air.

"Calm down guys, calm down! I fell down... that's all," explained Albert, getting up to turn off the alarm.

"Oh, really? That's all?" retorted Ruth, entering his room. She had only just jumped out bed, but her long red hair still looked perfectly brushed. "Next time please make sure to knock over the other half of the bedroom so you can wake up the neighbors too." She set on the edge of his bed.

"Don't make a big deal out of it. It was already time for us to wake up. Besides..." Albert stopped for a moment, glancing at the sky one more time. "You have no idea what just happened. The sky was red a few minutes ago. Totally red."

"You need to stop watching those scary movies, Albert," advised Ruth.

"It has nothing to do with movies..." Albert denied.

"Yes, it does. Horror movies make you lose your sense of what's real," said Victor, placing the tennis racket on the floor. "So, was it the same dream again?"

Albert nodded, then turned to face a drawing on the wall. He grabbed a pencil on his nightstand and carefully retouched the thick eyebrow of the face that kept appearing on his dreams. "Yeah... same situation and that same guy..."

"Did he say something different this time?" asked Sarah, intrigued.

"No, Mom, but... when I saw the red sky, I heard his voice in my head... saying... Gaia."

"I'm starting to get worried about you, kid." Victor passed his hand through Albert's hair. "Go get dressed for school. I'll go take a shower..."

"Today is the big day!" celebrated Sarah, kissing Victor.

"You are going to watch the ceremony, right honey?" Victor locked Sarah in his arms.

"I'd never miss out on my hubby getting a medal from the mayor!" she replied.

"Astronomer of the Year!" exclaimed Ruth, picking up

a crumpled newspaper page from the nightstand and pointing to a photo of Victor. "Sounds pretty huge, Dad, so huge that I should be going too."

"You are going to school, young lady!" stated Victor, leaving the room.

"So, Mom…" Ruth pulled her mother down to sit next to her on the bed. "Can I move downstairs now that Albert is losing his mind? I could seriously have a stroke next time he wakes me up like that."

Ruth's exaggerated tone provoked a laugh from Sarah, but it trailed off as soon as she noticed Albert's anguished expression. "You know, son, your grandpa told me about 'red skies'…"

Sarah never hid her fascination with her father. She always proudly described him as intelligent and caring, deeply in tune with nature. Sadly, she had lost her parents at a young age, but she carried on their love for all living things, tending to her garden and volunteering at several animal shelters.

"My dad used to say that red skies are a sign that big things are coming…" Sarah continued.

"Big things are coming? That sounds good! Maybe girls will finally let you talk to them, Bro…" Ruth gave him a punch on the shoulder.

"Maybe…" Albert smiled, thinking of the possibilities.

"The sooner you get dressed, the sooner you'll find out.

Gaia could be the name of the lucky girl!" Sarah encouraged him, flashing her contagious smile.

"The lucky nerd girl..." retorted Ruth, leaving the bedroom to get ready.

Two

Soap was lying on the living room floor. His ears rose at the sound of a door opening behind him. He quickly turned around to see who might be invading his territory: Sarah, Ruth and Albert. The dog gnawed contentedly on his rubber ball, as if inviting the group to play. Albert, depleted of energy, briskly caressed the dog's head.

"Cheer up, Albert!" said Ruth.

"I was thinking... these *big things,* could they be for the worse?" asked Albert.

He flashed back to his day at school, which could be summarized by the following:

1. Just after he entered the school building, someone splattered an entire cup of instant noodles on his hair. Another boy volunteered to help him cleaning and activated a fire extinguisher over him. Very effective.

2. After complaining, he somehow found himself hanging by his underwear from the cafeteria door.

3. Putting all that behind him, and changing into an

emergency sweatshirt, he decided to take the first step in his master plan for asking out a girl from his homeroom. His "so what are you up to this weekend?" was met with a look of pity and fear far worse than any "no."

4. At the end of the day, he was hit in the face by a soccer ball while taking a short-cut through a PE class. The perfect ending.

"I'm sure something good is going to happen for you, son..." Sarah consoled him. "Maybe tomorrow, maybe next week..."

"Hope it's at least this year," said Albert. "Or I'll be spending all my free time in the library's self-help aisle."

"Victor, are you feeling okay?" Sarah asked, drawing Albert's attention.

Victor was pacing from side to side in the middle of the room, visibly agitated. His shirt was not perfectly tucked in as usual, but half unbuttoned and wrinkled. His frowning forehead exposing some wrinkles and leaving him with a worried expression. "You were late today..." complained Victor.

"Well, you were early!" replied Sarah. "We ended up having some pizza, since you've said that you didn't want to celebrate the prize you won today... you just wanted to 'enjoy your telescope'..."

"Yeah, you have a weird way of having fun, Dad. Didn't you observe your planets after the ceremony?" Ruth sprang to the sofa.

"Yes, I did. That's the problem I guess..."

"What are you talking about?" asked Sarah, kissing Victor on his forehead. "Are you sick? Your skin is as cold as ice..."

Victor mumbled something incomprehensible.

"Honey, why don't you sit down and tells us what's going on?" Sarah suggested. "Ruth, please get some tea to calm your father down!"

Ruth rushed to the kitchen and returned briskly, handing her father the drink. The hot liquid disappeared in one gulp, and Victor's trembling hand returned the glass.

Sarah took Victor's hands and pulled him down to the couch.

"Something very odd happened at work today," Victor began, with a trembling voice.

"What happened, Dad? Did you get fired?" asked Albert, sitting beside him.

In life, there were some people who would see their job as just a way to survive. But there were also those who considered their jobs as the core of their identity. The job defined who they were. His dad was one of those people. His feelings, motivations and behaviors would always be directly linked to his performance at work. A simple mistake had the power to ruin his mood for weeks or even months. Success was the only key to his happiness.

"No, I didn't get fired..." replied Victor. "Actually, I made a remarkable discovery."

"That's wonderful," said Sarah affectionately. She struggled to meet her husband's eyes.

"However...science..." Victor searched for the words. "I'm afraid to... reveal... that it's unrealistic, almost supernatural, you might say."

"Dad, please calm down and help us understand why you're so nervous," asked Albert, trying to connect the dots.

Victor nodded and leaned forward. "It turns out that, when I was just about ready to pack up for the evening, I saw what appeared to be an unrecorded planet: tiny, green and beautiful. It's situated between Earth and Mars but it appeared to come and go. I've checked all publications to see if anyone has ever mentioned this celestial body before..."

"And..." Ruth tried to control her excitement. She could already see her dad's photo in the front page of every newspaper and magazine.

"Nobody has! I just can't explain it. I wouldn't even believe it myself if I hadn't seen it with my own eyes and rechecked with every telescope and instrument at the planetarium."

"Victor, that's amazing," Sarah celebrated. "Did you share your discovery with anyone?

"No, I did not," Victor answered sharply. "I don't want

to be labeled a 'nut case', and lumped together with people who say they were kidnapped by UFOs. I need more evidence to substantiate what I saw before reporting the discovery or publishing a paper..." His thoughts started to drift. "How could I be the only one?

"Because you're special," replied a familiar voice.

Everyone turned in panic. Soap's barking instantly rang out in the direction of the stranger, but suspiciously ceased as fast as it had begun started. Soap gently approached the man as if he was an old friend.

"Who the hell are you? How did get inside our house?" Victor shot back, his hand reaching for his cell phone.

"My name is Julius Alsky, but please, just call me Julius. I apologize for intruding like this, but the door was open," he said with a smile, attempting to lighten the tense mood. "I have the answer." The intruder looked directly at Victor as if he were the only person in the room.

"What in God's name are you talking about? How do you know my name?" Victor rose and began moving towards the man, trying not to seem intimidated.

"I know you!" Albert interrupted, calmly rising to position himself between the man and his father. "You're the guy who keeps appearing in my dreams!"

"He is! He's the man on that drawing you made!" Sarah exclaimed in shock.

Ruth carefully approached the stranger and analyzed

his face "Yeah... There's no doubt about it..."

"How is that possible?" wondered an even more intrigued Victor.

"Do you mean the tsunami dream?" Julius asked with a grin on his face.

Albert nodded.

"You had a Revelation... and that's a great gift!" Julius gave an awkward pat on Albert's shoulder. "We can only proceed with our invitation when someone from the family has the *key dream*. That's when we know that you really are special."

"Revelation?" Albert repeated. He wanted answers, not more puzzles to decipher.

"It's a kind of warning; each dream has a different meaning. Yours was about you and your family leaving Earth for a place reserved for the Chosen," said Julius, sitting on the couch, while the Kleins remained standing, speechless.

A long silence filled the room.

"Leave Earth?" Albert wanted to make sure he had heard it right.

"Hold on here," Victor intervened, with an angrier tone. "First of all, no one in my family is going anywhere. Secondly, I demand that you explain who you are and what you're doing to my son..."

"Should you choose to stay, I'll respect your decision,

Mr. Klein," Julius cut him off, adding a smile to his response.

"Where are we going?" asked Ruth, wondering what she might be able to buy there.

"To Gaia," said Julius.

The Kleins looked at each other. The mystery word.

"What did you say?" Victor softened his tone.

"Gaia?" repeated Albert, sitting on the couch, feeling like he no longer had control of his own body. It was all so surreal, and he was too practical to accept that this could actually be happening.

"That's right. Gaia is the name of the planet you saw today," Julius confirmed.

"Well, at least it proves Albert's not crazy... and neither is Dad..." Ruth said to lighten the atmosphere.

"So the planet really exists?" asked Sarah.

"Absolutely," Julius confirmed. "The planet remains invisible to those who are unprepared."

"Is this some kind of joke?" Victor continued searching in his mind for possible security lapses at the observatory. "It must be someone from the office who..."

"I can assure you that we never joke about these matters. We allowed your discovery of Gaia – you were ready. With your permission, let me explain everything."

Julius stood up and threw a small green square in the

air. It stayed there, suspended. He slid his fingers through the object, increasing it to the size of a television.

"Gaia is approximately one-fifth the size of Earth, but with similar gravity." As Julius started his speech, the image of a small, emerald-colored, planet, protected by what seemed to be a bubble, was projected by the object like an impressive 3-D movie. "Its surface is composed of 85% percent water and 15% land." The device zoomed in on the planet, showing a land mass in the shape of a spider, surrounded by crystal waters. "Gaia also contains four main islands, all ecological reserves of the highest beauty. Only 2 million inhabitants reside on the planet."

Julius took a pause, as if checking to see if everyone was still following. The Kleins' curiosity had been piqued and was swelling with each new phrase.

"In terms of development, Gaia is light-years ahead of Earth. Our ancestors strove to create an environment where science, nature and the mysteries of life would be inextricably linked; a world where peace and harmony are achievable. At certain moments in history, our world opens the door to select individuals from distant lands. This is one of those moments. As one of the planet's main coordinators, I was sent as a special ambassador to welcome you."

"What makes us so special?" questioned Ruth, her green eyes narrowing in a mixture of curiosity and suspicious.

"Most importantly, you possess our ideals," summarized Julius. "We have no doubt Mr. Klein's vast knowledge and intellectual curiosity would help our understanding of the universe. Sarah's kindness and respect for nature is already well known among your own people. Ruth and Albert have inherited a rare combination of reason and intuition. Traits like yours we welcome, love and respect in our world. For these reasons, the door has been opened for all of you."

Julius decreased the size of his device and turned it off.

"I have no idea what to say," Sarah confessed, sitting next to Albert on the couch, completely delighted with the description.

"How did you find us? I mean, how could you know so much about us if you live on Gaia?" Albert asked.

"Liaisons from Gaia are stationed here on Earth," Julius revealed. "They are common people, scattered in select countries. They have been monitoring you."

"This is all very intriguing, to say the least," said Victor. "But I'm not willing to accept this 'opportunity'..."

"Then I'm afraid you will lose the chance to change your lives forever; to reside in the ideal world of your dreams; to raise your children in health and in peace. Gaia is a land which seems magical, but it's real." As he ended his speech, Julius scanned the eyes of the Klein family individually.

Sarah turned to Victor, and addressed him in her

sweetest tone. "Honey... you know, I've always hoped to live in a place where we know nothing could harm our family. How could we deny our son and daughter the chance to be truly happy?"

"But we are happy!" Victor responded bluntly.

"Are we? I was just a few minutes late tonight and you were already worried," continued Sarah. "We're always worried about the kids staying out late alone... Do you remember how you felt after the neighbors were robbed? Our family's welfare should be our top priority."

"And safety shouldn't be your only concern..." continued Julius. "Would you prevent your family from strengthening their immune systems to a point where no virus or bacteria could affect their bodies? Victor, would you toss away the chance to spend many more years alive and healthy with your family? The life expectancy of an inhabitant of Gaia is around two hundred years."

Victor's expression proved that he was starting to agree with Sarah, but he wasn't the type of person who gave up on an argument so easily.

"If we go, don't you think people will wonder what happened to us?" he argued, crossing his arms.

"We'll take care of that," Julius intervened. "We'll insert memories in the minds of those who have had contact with you throughout your lives. They'll believe that you have traveled to another country. Every time they think about calling you, they'll immediately change their minds."

"Does that mean that I'll have to leave all my friends behind?" asked Ruth, showing some reluctance.

Victor immediately turned to Sarah, as though ready to make a point. "See! They have their friends here!"

"I don't," said Albert. In a minute he relived all the lonely moments he'd ever had; the birthday parties that nobody attended, the trips and get-togethers that he was never invited to, the games that he was picked for last.

"Ruth, happiness sometimes requires sacrifice," said Julius.

"Julius is right, Ruth," said Sarah. "Besides, you can make friends anywhere!"

"But…" Victor took a long and deep breath. He could see that his family was already coming to a decision, but he had to at least make sure that they wouldn't end up falling into a trap. "What if, after a few days on Gaia, we decide to return to Earth?"

"Then further precautions would necessarily follow," Julius replied. He stared out the back window at the star-filled sky. "I'd be forced to make you disappear completely."

The eyes and mouths of the Kleins fell open as they turned to each other.

Julius exploded with laughter. "Sorry, I couldn't resist," he continued as his laughter dissipated to a trickle. "There is a period of 30 days in which you can decide whether to stay or leave Gaia. Should you decide to leave, no one, including yourselves, would ever remember your absence."

"How can we be assured that we'd be allowed to return in 30 days if we change our minds? What if we experience physical problems as a result of this experiment?" Victor questioned.

"You will simply have to trust me," Julius stated. "Thirty days is the limit. After that, we can't guarantee anything."

The family again sat in silence. Only Soap's breathing was audible, as he had long since fallen asleep under the spell of Julius's voice.

"Thirty days sounds good to me," said Ruth, finally. "Let's think of it as a vacation that we might not remember!"

"That's the perfect answer. Very reasonable, actually. Don't think you are leaving your lives behind, just taking a few days off to discover a new and better world. That's it." Julius rested his case and waited for the verdict.

"I wanna go too," Albert opined, looking at his mom as though asking for back up.

"I don't want to lose the opportunity to discover this ideal place he's talking about, where they appreciate everything that I value," Sarah concluded.

All eyes turned in Victor's direction.

"Well… I'm far from sure about this," said Victor.

"But I don't want to be the bad guy who vetoes it... and... I guess I can use some vacation..."

"I'm glad that you all made the right decision." Julius smiled, in triumph.

Julius threw his device in the air one more time. It stayed suspended, in its original size. "Please don't close your eyes and don't blink too much..." he ordered.

Sarah grasped her husband's tense hand tightly and sympathetically glanced at the twins to record one last mental photograph before their great but uncertain transformation.

Before the family had the chance to say anything, the device flashed like a strobe light faster and faster until nobody could see anything.

Julius's voice rang out from the blurring and silence.

"Welcome to Gaia".

Three

"It's so... so... beautiful," Sarah whispered, her eyes glazed over in shock.

"This, my honored guests, is your new home!" Julius opened his arms, like a proud magician who had performed the most spectacular trick.

A bright and beautiful moon radiated above a large brick house situated in a spacious yard. As the Kleins realized what had just occurred, they couldn't hide their amazement. Even Soap was wobbly and confused.

"What... what happened?" Victor sat on the floor, dizzy with wonder. His attention was drawn to a strange full moon, bright but smaller. "I've never imagined... It's a totally different angle of the lunar surface. It's simply... unbelievable! And what about that...?" He noticed another celestial body close to the moon, much larger and more colorful. "Is that... Is that... Earth?"

"Wow!" exclaimed Ruth and Albert simultaneously.

"So Gaia is near the Earth after all... " murmured Albert tilting his head at a sharp angle, transfixed by the spectacular view.

"Indeed." Julius smiled. "Shall we enter?"

The family followed Julius towards the narrow path through the colossal garden that surrounded the house, illuminated by circular floating lights and the sky's natural brilliance. The yard alone, calculated Albert, exceeded more than ten times the size of their whole residence on Earth. Despite the obscure darkness, Soap suddenly appeared several feet in front, whining and sniffing around the base of their new home, treading cautiously.

Approaching the large palatial door, Albert's eyes unsuccessfully scanned its surface for a doorknob. The door suddenly swung open by itself.

"Who has the remote control?" asked Albert, glancing at the hands of everyone on the porch.

"The door opens itself when you approach," explained Julius.

"I'm just wondering how it can differentiate between us and..." started Victor, but he was immediately cut off by his daughter.

"Our dog sleeps more than he watches," said Ruth, ignoring her father's usual expression of concern. "I'm sorry, dad. You were saying that..."

"You are completely safe in Gaia," Julius reminded them in a reassuring and patriotic voice. "There has never been a serious crime here for more than two hundred years."

"That sounds like utopia. There must have been at least one incident," said Sarah in disbelief.

"The evolution of any society cannot only be scientific," explained Julius. "It must be accompanied by moral development. Gaians value, above all, moral principles and ethical living."

The front door opened to a cozy living room with furniture and paintings that were similar to the Klein's residence on Earth. The family could see that Julius and his aides had done everything to make them feel at home and not in a strange new environment.

Pots with beautiful plants were in the corners of the room. Following the intense and sweet fragrance, Sarah reached out for a red rose.

"Insane, right mom?" interjected Albert after watching the rose pass through Sarah's hand. "They're perfect holograms, like a sci-fi movie!"

Some moving images of important events from the Kleins' life took up an entire wall of the room. These 'memory videos' were soon replaced by others in a continuous motion, including important events like the Klein's wedding; the twin's birth, and Albert getting hit with a soccer ball at school on different occasions. On the other walls, they found another surprise. The yard was visible from the inside of the house as if the walls were invisible or made of glass.

"How is that possible?" Ruth broke in, scrutinizing

each wall. "From the outside, brick; from inside, glass! The walls are transparent!" she yelled in amazement.

"How exactly is that accomplished?" asked a perplexed Victor.

"The bricks are nothing more than a privacy-projection," said Julius. "Many Gaian advancements, Mr. Klein, will no doubt test the limited concepts you are accustomed to on Earth."

"Everything is so perfect," said Sarah, and as she peeked through the dining room her amazement increased.

"Stairs? Is that what it is?" asked Ruth, a little confused at the large wood staircase that was located in the corner of the room. "I would've thought a house like this would have a high-tech elevator or something."

"Well we tried to adapt the house to what you're used to, but there is a 'high-tech elevator' as you say, right beside the stairs. Can you see that circle?" Julius pointed at a small green circle on the floor. "You just need to get on top of that spot in order to..."

Julius interrupted his sentence, realizing that Ruth had already disappeared after stepping on the green circle.

"We're definitely interested in what's upstairs now..." Albert walked towards the circle, waiting for permission from Julius to step into it.

"First room on the right," said Julius, waving him forward.

After walking through a long hallway full of paintings and strange devices, Ruth and Albert finally arrived at the doorway to a bedroom. There was a long silence. They stood frozen, as if time itself stood still.

The room contained an enormous bed, two paintings and one nightstand. Nothing else. They turned to Julius as if expecting him to perform another magic trick. He didn't. A look of disappointment began to slowly spread across Albert's face. He remembered the exact same feeling from Christmas Day two years ago, when he and Ruth had wanted mountain bikes but had received an old and used pair of skates each instead.

"Well?" asked Julius, having fun with his little game.

"Well... do you want to know the truth?" said Ruth in an embarrassed tone. But she could not contain her increasing disappointment. "It doesn't even have a closet! How can I live without a closet? We've got to go shopping! And there's no television. Or stereo. And only one bed! Sharing a room is one thing, but sharing a bed with Albert...? Impossible!"

"Actually this will be Albert's room..." began Julius.

"Ha! See Albert, you get the room with nothing!" said Ruth. She moved aside to let Albert pass.

"But all the rooms are the same..." continued Julius, making everyone else laugh. "Let me clarify something. You may transform your room as you desire. For example: 'Wall color: blue'; 'Change painting: Albert Einstein'."

The walls flashed into a deep blue, and the famous scientist's portrait replaced the painted landscape.

"Now that could make you instantly rich back on Earth!" said a surprised Victor.

"Don't forget that the window is also an optical illusion. You may increase or decrease its size." Julius then turned to Ruth. "Do you see the gaps on the walls?"

"Is it a modern mini-fireplace?" asked Ruth, approaching the gap.

"It's a built-in wardrobe, you could say. The 'gap' is where you pick up clothes or return them after. The wardrobe employs a self-cleaning technology; it washes and arranges everything that you have returned in seconds. If you get closer to the gap, a menu will appear with..."

"Options? There are options for mattresses?" interrupted Albert, sitting on the bed and checking out the virtual menu. "This is freaking me out! Check it out dad!"

"Air, water, grass, sand, gel..." continued Albert. "I don't even know what to choose! Julius, you must be..."

"Kidding!" interrupted a desperate Ruth. "You must be kidding that I'll have to use these as... clothes."

The wardrobe-menu was showing as its contents large quantities of some sort of clear plastic fabric only. No trendy jackets, summer dresses, or even accessories. Just fabric squares.

"The clothes are also transformed as you desire, they

can take any form and style," said Julius. "You'll design your own clothes."

"That's awesome, Julius!" yelled Ruth, anxious to try it out.

"Oh, crap…" Albert knew he would have a hard time with that sort of thing; he had no talent for matching clothes, much less designing them.

"You'll be fine…" assured Julius. "Well, I'll let you enjoy the house."

Before he exited the room, Sarah grasped both his hands. She looked at him and before the first tear dropped, she managed to say a few words. "Thanks, Julius… We simply love it."

Albert was lying awake on his bed, completely absorbed in his thoughts. He had adjusted his bedroom's wall and the ceiling to transparent mode, and was fascinated by the birds flying overhead and the squirrels visiting the trees next door.

Everything happened so fast… the dreams, the red-sky, Julius's visit, the new home… a day ago he was feeling completely worn out, with no hope for an interesting life, and now there he was, discovering a whole planet he could never have imagined. That was definitely more than the change he was waiting for, and he couldn't be more eager to explore its each and every detail.

"Hello! Good Morning!" an unfamiliar voice resonated throughout the room, making Albert jump up from his bed.

"There were three complete strangers in his bedroom: a short blonde woman in her forties, an athletic dark-skinned man, and a teenage boy. They were all looking in his direction.

Albert stood still, petrified. He stared at the intruders for a while, awaiting further explanation. Nothing.

"Who are you? What are you doing in my bedroom?" Albert gathered some courage to ask.

"We're your neighbors, the Beckers..." began the lady. "Seems that Julius forgot to explain how the intercom works... it projects guests' images into whatever room is occupied."

"Oh, okay... got it! You're using the intercom then!" Albert said.

Albert passed his fingers through the visitors, confirming their images were nothing but another perfect hologram. But then something else hit him: his clothes. He had designed his pajamas pants with stamps of... models... pretty models... in swimsuits. His face went instantly red.

"Just so you know, the bikini girls... I mean, the artistic models... on my pants..." Albert racked his brain to come up with an explanation. "I was trying to experiment with the capabilities of the fabric design... mechanism..."

"We can't see you... we only hear your voice..." said

the man, trying to hide his amusement.

Strong laughter echoed through the house. Ruth's laugh, Albert recognized. He quickly realized that since the guests' images were projected in all occupied rooms, his family had been listening to his awkward performance from the beginning.

"I hope you're not in the bathroom, though," said the teenage stranger, breaking into laughter.

"Oh... no... I'm not..." Albert struggled to regain his composure. "Sorry, we weren't expecting any visitors... see you downstairs in a minute."

The front door was already open when Albert came out in shorts and a t-shirt, and he could recognize the faces from his bedroom minutes ago. Soap had noticed the Beckers long before, while digging in the garden, but he only now had the courage to cautiously sniff the guests' feet.

"Good morning! Please come in," said Sarah, stepping politely aside to allow the Becker family to pass.

Albert, Ruth and Victor stood behind, watching with intense interest.

"I, for one, am relieved," said the woman, taking Sarah's hand. "We've been waiting for another Chosen family for some time now. I'm Sophia Becker; this is my husband George; and our son, Nicolaus."

"Nice to meet you all. I'm Sarah Klein, this is my husband Victor, and these are my kids, Albert and Ruth."

"Let me guess..." Nicolaus approached Albert for a handshake. The boy looked a lot like his dad, except for his height and posture. "They named you in honor of Albert Einstein?"

"Yep..." responded Albert, shaking the boy's hand.

"My dad named me after Copernicus..." said Nicolaus, while Soap sniffed him over.

"Please stop bothering our guests, Soap." Ruth leaned down and took the dog in her arms.

"Soap?" Nicolaus smiled. "And this name is in honor of what specifically?"

"Powdered soap," answered Ruth. "When he was a puppy he ate almost a whole box."

"So you're also a Chosen family?" asked Victor, intrigued.

"We left Earth five years ago and we've never regretted our decision," said George. "It seems that we have a lot in common..."

"Julius told us that you're an astronomer," Sophia cut her husband off. "George was one of NASA's best scientists!" she said proudly.

"Wow that's great!" exclaimed Victor.

"We'll have time to catch up later," George said as he tapped Victor's shoulder. "Now I'm afraid we have to attend to a request made by none other than Julius himself."

"How would you all like a grand tour of Gaia?" Sophia rubbed her hands together, in excitement.

"A tour? I haven't even finished touring my bedroom, but I'm in," said Albert.

The whole Klein family agreed, in a crescendo of enthusiasm.

"Great!" Sophia celebrated. "Julius said that a breakfast basket will be waiting for us on the Flyer."

"You'll understand what that is in a little while..." said Nicolaus, anticipating their questions.

"Now, where's your garage?" asked Sophia.

"To be honest, I have no idea..." said Victor, almost afraid to get lost in his huge residence.

"Do we have a car?" asked Albert, while he fantasized about what a Gaian vehicle would look like.

"Not exactly... Come on, I'll show you." George started walking to the back of the house. "Gaian houses usually have the same basic floor plan; it won't be hard to find."

George led the Klein family to a door by a cupboard in the dining room. As they passed through the door, the steps of a spiral staircase appeared and then disappeared with each step they took.

The garage was the most futuristic part of the house: circular and simulating a nocturnal sky illuminated only by the moon; so perfect that they all could swear that they were floating.

A large transparent capsule lay horizontally in the center of the garage, totally empty.

"Here you are!" said George, smiling. He walked around inspecting the capsule.

"It's just like ours, but we have the ocean as our theme instead of a night sky," shared Nicolaus, sounding undecided about which he preferred.

"I think it's... beautiful," said Sarah, straining to identify a constellation.

"Quite different from our garage on Earth," Victor finally observed. He had a number of questions that he knew would have to wait.

"We had a bunch of junk in our garage... including the car," said Ruth.

"I take it this capsule is our car, then," Albert moved closer and extended a finger towards the transparent object.

"Not quite, Albert... it provides access to your transportation, actually," said Sophia, finding the Kleins' confusion quite amusing.

George stepped up beside his wife. "What we call a Zoom is the main form of transportation on Gaia. It travels through an underground system of interconnected garages: commercial, residential and even farms."

"So it's a subway?" asked Victor.

"You could say that," George replied, as he ran his hand along the capsule, "But a Zoom is capable of extreme velocities. It can also transport any number of passengers."

"You just need to adjust the configuration to activate your request," said Sophia, eager to perform a demonstration. "Look!"

As Sophia approached the capsule, a small screened popped up and she typed in the number of passengers desired.

Seven colorful seats took shape inside the capsule.

"The Zoom will take us to the Tour Center. And then we'll use a Flyer to see Gaia," Nicolaus informed them.

"I am totally lost with all this," interrupted Ruth. "My brain doesn't move as fast as these vehicles."

Sophia placed a comforting hand on Ruth's shoulder. "Think of it as an airbus, but oddly the slowest form of transportation we have. Enough talking for now," she blurted out impatiently. "Let's go guys!"

"What about Soap?" asked Albert. The dog perked up from Ruth's lap at the sound of his name.

"Of course he can go," Sophia authorized, entering the capsule.

Albert followed Sophia and took a seat on the first row. He closed his eyes and began making mental calculations to estimate their arrival time at the Tour Center. Nicolaus nudged him a second later. They had already arrived.

FOUR

The Kleins rose from their seats, amazed. Rather than a modern and automated mall, the Tour Center was like an immense garden under an open sky, with crystal lakes full of fish, flowers of every imaginable color, gracefully pruned trees of varying species, and birds shooting around in every direction. Albert struggled to restrain Soap, anxious from the dozens of other dogs milling about the Center. The birds passing at every conceivable angle heightened his desire to break free.

Passersby greeted them with genuine affection – smiling and reaching out to shake their hands. The large crowd at the Center surprised Albert; he was worried he would run into green people with several heads. The familiar faces dispelled his doubts while at the same time creating others: what were their lives like? What were their concerns? Desires? Goals? Personalities? Who were the Gaians really, besides just creative people wearing all sorts of colorful clothes?

"This place is amazing!" said Albert. "A little different from what I'd imagined, though. Where are the modern buildings? This is like a huge garden..."

"Let me put it this way," replied Sophia. "Imagine a rich but very modest family. Gaia is like that. They have all of this wealth and advanced technology, but the population has a simple lifestyle. More connected with nature."

"Everyone seems so happy here!" noted Sarah.

"That's because we *are* happy," said Sophia, smiling.

"Our only worry is having nothing to worry about!" added George, before pointing them to a bench less than a hundred yards. "The Flyer is right over there."

"Sure, you can see the bench. But even that will disappear once you're seated," said Nicolaus.

"What's the point of being invisible?" Albert wondered.

"To avoid visual pollution. It's against the Gaian Code to disturb the sky. The Flyer also transmits a sound that is imperceptible to us, but not to the birds, so they don't get hit," explained Sophia.

"I wonder if there're more people like us here... I mean Chosen families," said Ruth, walking slowly. She could've stayed at the center for hours, just admiring it.

"Only a few, or we wouldn't be called Chosen ones," said Nicolaus.

"The selection process is very rigorous..." George turned to Victor. "Hey man, you don't look as excited as your family... Something wrong?"

"Everything seems great, don't get me wrong..." said Victor. "It's just that, why do they choose the so-called most advanced people to live here? I mean, Earth's most capable inhabitants should remain there. Earth needs strong leaders who can help the planet develop..."

"But the Chosen are helping Earth's evolution," said George. "We have a few programs to..." George lost his train of though. His attention was drawn to a peculiar message left on the Flyer's bench – digital graffiti projected by a small gadget in form of a synthetic flame.

As the whole group approached the Flyer, a look of surprise crossed their faces.

Albert blinked, hoping he had misread. But the message couldn't be clearer:

"Please don't stay. Freedom to Earth! Freedom to Gaia!"

"What the heck..." Sophia crossed her arms, in indignation.

"This is Gaian's freedom of speech in action," said a man in dark clothes with deep dark eyes. He was just a few steps from the bench, using a device identical to the one that Julius had used on Earth. "This traditional 'tour' seems to be a good opportunity for people to express their opinion. I took some pictures to add to our files..."

The man walked towards the group.

"I'm Lionel Kirk," he continued. "I work for the Council in the Integration Department. This kind of protest is very common during the Chosen's initial 30 days on Gaia. Some Gaians argue that Gaia interfering with Earth is un-ethical. They want independence and freedom..."

"I can't say I disagree," said Victor. "Earth should have freedom from interference and freedom to choose, regard-less of the course the planet eventually takes."

"Exactly," said Lionel, after a cold look at Victor. "And Gaia should be free from the Chosen. That's what some people think."

"So there are Gaians who disagree with the 'Integration' process?" questioned Sarah.

"Since Ulysses became the Council President, things have changed significantly. The majority of Gaians supports the directives of the Integration Department and also ap-proves of the aid to Earth," said Lionel, in monotone voice. "Well... my job here is done. I'm heading out."

Lionel grabbed the small projector, turned his back to the group and walked away quickly, leaving behind a quiet and disturbed pair of Chosen families.

Albert's head was spinning. What was that guy talking about? And what would be the meaning of that message? He always appreciated truth and honesty, but he knew very well how hurtful words could be. He simply wasn't pre-pared for all of that now. He had great expectations, and hoped he wouldn't end up with even greater disappoint-ment.

"Is it just me or was that guy very rude?" Ruth broke the silence, while taking a seat on the bench as if nothing was ever projected on it. "Seriously, he said he's from the Integration Department but he didn't even welcome us!"

"Lionel is just not a people-person," said George. "But let's forget about it! We don't want anything or anyone to spoil your first day here." He took a seat next to Ruth.

"And neither does Julius!" added Sophia. "Look at the basket he prepared for our tour!"

Sophia grabbed the glass basket that was lying on the floor and carefully put it on the top of the bench. After sitting right next to it, she opened the basket by pressing a small and delicate button on its surface. She took off the red cloth, and showed the colorful contents to everyone: fruits, cakes and juices.

"It looks delicious, but I thought we would have some kind of futuristic food!" said Ruth.

"Gaia's food is very similar to the food on Earth," explained Sophia, handing out small bottles of juice. "What's different is the way they grow the food. What I refer to as the art of food: understanding its energy."

The Kleins quickly served themselves. They had been so excited the night before that they had forgotten to even eat dinner, and now their stomachs were rumbling in complaint. As they started to chew the food, they couldn't hide their amazement.

"I've never had a cake like this!" said Albert, intrigued by how the flavor seemed to multiply after each bite.

"I remember saying that a lot: 'never seen this', 'never seen that'..." commented Nicolaus. "I'll *never* forget!"

"I have to admit I really *never* have had a breakfast like this!" added Sarah, savoring some grapes.

"I've *never* even liked fruit!" joked Ruth, tearing into one of the shiny blue apples.

"You poor darling!" Sophia patted Soap's head. The dog was already drooling, hoping for some distraction to grab anything he could. "Julius sent some special 'food' for you too!" Sophia revealed an oddly curved bone that instantly disappeared into the dog's mouth. "Believe me, this is nothing but simple dog food," she said, turning to Sarah. "The taste and the form are just to please the dog. I chose one with chamomile to calm him down when we take off."

"I just set up the Flyer!" said George to Sophia. "Don't worry, I chose an amazing tour route! Buckle up guys, here we go!"

As the Flyer began its gradual ascent, the benches and the floor disappeared. Soap groaned in fear and jumped into Albert's lap.

"It's a very intriguing vehicle this Flyer..." commented Victor. "Would like to know more about its structure later..."

George nodded in agreement; after all, he could understand the way a scientist's mind worked.

The Tour Center faded in the distance and lovely, colorful houses, started to appear. On each roof top was a drawing, and viewed together they looked like comic strips. Entire neighborhoods displayed whimsical and eccentric scenes: ballet dancers fighting against gigantic ants, clothes on strike for less washing, an aquaphobic fish trying to walk, food rebelling against sharp knives, and so on.

"Remember, those are projections," said Sophia. "Residents are encouraged to be creative. Many of these houses will look different next week, and they'll tell a different story."

Gaia had no lamp posts, no traffic lights, no cars, and not even streets; only sidewalks connected the houses, surrounded by wooded and flowery parks. Viewed from above, Gaia looked like one massive, peaceful rural village.

The Flyer passed through mountainous valleys, breathtaking beaches with bright white sand and crystalline water, island wildlife preserves, and huge farms with geometrical plantations.

Though they all felt that they wanted it to last forever, the tour ended in just a few hours. But that wasn't such bad news after all, thought Albert, he still had his own house to tour, and that experience could be even better.

The Kleins took the rest of the day to enjoy and explore the house. But first, Sarah assigned Albert and Ruth two important tasks: feeding Soap and giving him a bath.

The first was easy. Soap had already been fed, they found out. On the porch, right next to the front door, a container released food from time to time. The nutritious meals were *camouflaged* as delicious human sweets, such as cake, ice-cream and even chocolate.

Such foods though weren't sufficient to rid the dog of his natural fear of water. Soap was keen not only to their intonation but also to their physical gestures around bath time. He therefore decided to make use of his one powerful ally: the enormous yard. For nearly an hour, Soap managed to escape the clutches of Albert and Ruth, running swiftly through the grass and hiding strategically behind plants, bushes and trees.

Yet these delaying tactics were no match for the modern devices of their new home. During one of his daring escapes, Soap wound up activating a remote sensor placed ingeniously beneath the illusory grass. On the next instant, Soap was swimming furiously in unfamiliar crystal-blue waters rather than running on secure ground. His shocked moan brought a roar of laughter from Albert and Ruth.

"You will not believe what I just found!" hollered Victor as he appeared from one corner of the house searching for the twins.

"A pool?" said Ruth, laughing in unison with Albert.

"Soap did us a big favor, Dad! I bet he regrets it now," said Albert, running to take hold of the dog's collar as he swam toward the pool's edge. Victor could only laugh.

"Bring that crazy dog over here," Victor commanded. "I located what looks like a dog bathing machine, inside of a flower-covered dog house, if you want to call it that. I'll show you guys!"

Victor headed back in the direction he had come, motioning for the twins to follow. After climbing up a small hill, they entered a compact house, still large enough to enter standing up. A low bed with scattered pillows filled the space, along with all sorts of dogs' toys.

"Look at your private room, Soap! That's awesome!" said Albert, struggling to maintain control of the dog, which was violently convulsing and kicking in his arms.

"Don't let him go, yet!" instructed Victor, leaning down and grabbing a weird device that looked more like a saddle. "This is what I found!" he said, looking at a puzzled Albert. "My scientific hunch says this is a dog-washing-machine!"

"*This* I have to see," said Ruth, unconvinced.

"Let's find out!" said Victor.

Victor placed the *saddle* on the frightened animal and it immediately began elastically stretching around his body. Only Soap's nose and eyes were now visible. The device turned red and a virtual screen appeared on top with a few options:

Quick cycle;
Full cycle;

Full cycle/massage.

Albert pressed the third option one, hoping to calm the distressed animal. The machine was immediately activated, followed by a low droning sound. Soap, looking like a superhero, fell into a hypnotic state for the next two minutes. Additional options then suddenly appeared:

Dry;

Dry/anti-allergic aroma;

Terminate cycle.

Without hesitating, Albert pressed the second option. Soap's offensive odor used to be detectable several rooms in advance. He sought to eliminate it once and for all.

The saddle began retracting and returned to its original size and color. Soap abruptly regained consciousness and sprang free from the washing area.

"Come here, my handsome baby!" said Ruth, overjoyed. "You're finally living up to your name, Soap! And look at your nails." She inspected every inch of his body.

Soap wagged his tail rapidly while his satisfied barks, one after another, echoed throughout the house.

"Think he liked his bath?" asked Albert rhetorically.

"From now on, he'll be up for daily showers," said Victor, contemplating the mysteries that awaited him in his human shower.

Ruth and Albert, as if on cue, both dashed toward the pool. It would quickly become their favorite part of the house. Like most Gaian devices, the pool offered various options such as sea water, freshwater or mineral water. The bottom surface could be transformed from grass, to sand, to rock, or any combination of dozens of options. The most impressive discovery, however, was the *cave option,* where they could find themselves swimming among small fishes in deep green water under crystalline rocks.

Meanwhile, Sarah was still trying to figure out how to use the appliances and locate the ingredients necessary for preparing a modest lunch.

As Sarah searched in vain for the stove, she found a curious display on the cupboard. After manipulating it on a whim, she couldn't help shouting Victor's favorite expression, "Eureka!"

The cupboard not only showed its digital cooking encyclopedia with hundred of options, but it also prepared any meal selected by Sarah in just a few minutes. When the food was already done, the living-room table set itself; its surface opening to reveal beautifully ordered ornate glasses and fine cutlery.

"I guess dinner is already ready!" said Sarah, smiling.

The family was called at once and assembled around the large yet cozy comfortable table. The exotic Gaian herbs lent an exquisite flavor to the meals.

Just before lunch came to an end, the image of Julius appeared on the dining-room wall.

"I must say, it's a superb afternoon," he said, in his deep voice, "I hope I didn't arrive at a bad time."

"Good afternoon, Julius! Please, come right into the dining room," said Sarah, hastily rising from her seat toward the front door to greet him. They returned a few moments later, entering the dining room together. Julius approached the table and swung his right hand forward from behind his back, displaying an object hidden beneath a colorful wrapping.

"What is it?" asked Ruth, grabbing the package. "Let me open it..."

"Thanks, Julius, but we don't want to get spoiled..." said Victor.

"I'm afraid we already are!" said Sarah. "The table sets itself, the cupboard cooks and does the dishes... the rooms clean themselves... It's the perfect house!"

"Brownies!" Ruth showed off the contents of the unwrapped package.

"Wow, you knew it already!" Albert aggressively reached across the table. "My favorite dessert ever!"

"I made them myself! I didn't use the cupboard. I hope you like it," said Julius.

"Well do join us at the table," said Sarah pointing to the free chair by her side. "C'mon, let's enjoy your gift together."

Julius politely accepted Sarah's invitation and took a

seat right next to Albert. After the family practically de-voured the tasty desert, he knew it was the perfect time to share his news.

"I'm glad you all had a wonderful time today with the Beckers and that you also enjoyed my dessert... but that's not why I'm here," Julius paused for a second, as if trying to create some suspense. "I'd like to give you these MODs - Microscopic Oricalco Devices." Julius handed a tiny trans-parent square device to each of them. "Tomorrow will be the first day of school for Ruth and Albert. You'll need these for sure."

The squares each measured less than one inch and weighed less than a sheet of paper.

"Is this thing just like the one that you used on Earth when you were telling us about Gaia?" asked Albert, in-specting it from every possible angle.

"With one exception: It doesn't allow any kind of inter-planetary travel. No Gaian is authorized to do so," said Jul-ius.

"So what exactly is an MOD?" questioned Victor.

"An MOD is a high-speed intelligent device made of microscopic particles of Oricalco, a self-assembling mineral compound. In a nutshell it performs many tasks; it's more than just a combination of computer-phone-television."

"Television?" asked Ruth, already curious about the TV shows.

"Yes, you just need to expend the size as your desire," said Julius.

In order to demonstrate the flexibility of the MOD, Julius slid the tip of his finger up and to the side of the mini-screen, enlarging the square to the size of a 70" TV.

"I must warn you that the experience can be a bit over-whelming at first," continued Julius. "The technology takes away your position as spectator, to integrate you as an additional character. You'll actually believe that you're living in all those films and cartoons."

"Cool!" approved Albert.

"What about me and Sarah?" Victor asked. "I'm assuming I'll start working tomorrow, right?"

"We have big plans for you both..." began Julius. "Sarah will be working with Sophia, researching floral compounds. And you, Victor, will work with research and exploration of planets and galaxies."

"I, for one, am ready to be useful!" Sarah declared, excited.

"Well, other galaxies do sound interesting," said Victor.

"But first you'll have to complete your studies," stated Julius.

"Well... you're well aware I received my PhD," said Victor. "I've lectured all over the entire country. I direct a world famous planetarium, and I've dedicated my life to research."

"Victor, we require a different kind of studies that are beyond your imagination. You will understand the history of Gaia, our secret science, the context of dreams, symbols, vital energy, numerology, astrology..."

"Dreams and numerology? I'm sorry, but there's no way I can take any of that seriously!" Victor shot a fiery glance toward Julius and for the first time his thoughts turned toward earth.

"Mr. Klein..." Julius took a long breath. "Gaia teaches much in the way of new possibilities. Some skepticism is difficult to overcome, but truth reveals itself in due time."

"Victor, what's wrong with trying something a little different?" asked Sarah, reaching for her husband's hand.

"Progress requires you to be free of prejudice," added Julius. "There is a reason we have these disciplines."

"Maybe I'm just not willing to start this whole process to become a citizen of Gaia," said Victor, leaning on the chair. "I still think that I'd be more useful on Earth, working to advance knowledge there."

"Honey, please think about our family's welfare," said Sarah, grasping his hand tightly.

"Come on, Dad. Give it a try," said Albert, confused by the awkward direction the conversation had taken. His dad's attitude didn't come as a total surprise, though.

Being away from friends on earth wouldn't be a problem for his dad, as he had none – only co-workers whose names he often forgot. Being away from relatives also wasn't a problem, as none were still alive – from a young age Victor had had to learn to depend on only his own efforts to be *someone* in life. But being away from work... well... that could become an issue. Albert couldn't recall the last time his dad had taken a vacation or even a sick day.

Not only that, but he had no other interests beyond work and science. Movies, sports, music and trips were completely absent from Victor's life. So to ask his father to stay away from the role that defined him was definitely too much. From now on, his dad would be a ticking time bomb. Patience was not one of his virtues and if they kept him away from his work for too long, the consequences could be disastrous.

"I'll give it a try for the next 28 days..." Victor finally stated. "That's all I can promise."

"Fair enough," said Julius, rising from the chair. "Then I shall see you and Sarah tomorrow. I volunteered to be your mentor."

FIVE

On The following day, Albert woke up anxious for school. Shouts echoed throughout the house when he discovered that his bed was nearly frozen. The temperature of the mattresses continued dropping until he was roused from sleep. Soap had tried earlier to wake him up with his tongue, but it was no match for the new alarm clock.

"School day..."Albert took a deep breath, while trying to figure out what to wear.

He was finally getting the hang of designing his clothes. First, he would have to choose the general format, such as top or bottom, shirt, pajamas, bathrobe, jacket, socks, cap, shoes, and etc. Then, he had to add its specification – for example, shorts, slacks, cargo pants, dress pants, sweatpants, etc, all completely adjustable. After that, he had to select the fabric: wool, leather, denim, wool, cotton, tweed, polyester, corduroy, fleece, spandex, leather plus names he'd never even heard of... And to finish, he could draw himself any print or choose between premade samples – geometric forms, wild animals, insects, electronic gadgets, funny phrases, cartoons, faces, etc.

"Time to make a great first impression," he said out loud.

He should stick to the basics, though. As he'd always heard, less was more. The last thing he wanted was to draw too much attention on his first day. Gray pants, white shirt and a black jacket would cut it.

He was trying very hard to not create any more expectations; after all, expectations were like windows to disappointment. But he couldn't help desiring things he hadn't had before... friends... popularity... girls... to feel that he fit in.

The graffiti message left on the bench was still on his mind... a reminder that the worst could actually happen. What if no one liked him? What if they treated him like an invader or a stupid foreigner?

Panic started overtaking his mind and he fought back to regain control. He needed to look calm and confident. Teenagers were probably pretty much the same everywhere, he thought, and they had the ability to detect fear in others' faces and actions.

Self-esteem was the key to evoke respect and admiration. "Time to enjoy life, instead of watching it pass by," said Albert. This mantra brought a smile to his face and he felt optimistic once again, ready for class.

This couldn't be their school. Before them was a huge circular area surrounded by trees, with an elegant entrance bordered by flower gardens. In the center of the giant circle stood a three story building made of light-colored wood. The well-manicured lawn was a deep green and resembled an ocean wave as it blew in the wind.

"Wow. It looks like a cottage from a fairytale," said Ruth as her eyes scanned the structure.

"Just wait until you see the other side," said Nicolaus, taking a few steps back to get a better view. "We better go to class now."

Many students had already arrived early and were seated on the lawn engaged in conversation. They appeared to all be looking in their direction, which brought a flush of red to the twin's faces. Ruth gathered her courage and put on a self-assured front proceeding behind the boys. But the unexpected happened to Albert.

Albert found himself trapped by some strong and unknown force that was dragging him towards the most perfect sight he had ever seen. As much as he tried, he couldn't break free from such intense blue eyes looking at him. His heart sped up, his legs trembled and he felt he had no control over his body. The girl's hypnotic beauty caused Albert to stumble over Nicolaus's heel and his face met the damp grass below with a thud.

Albert remained on the ground for what seemed like an eternity as the laughs of the other students echoed in his ears. Yet when he reopened his eyes, he realized these laughs were actually just shouts of concern from a small crowd that had gathered around him to help.

"Don't move him," ordered a tall boy, spreading his arms to the sides to form a protective barrier. "Are you okay?"

"Yeah, I... I think so," responded Albert, still imagining the angelic face which he still sought out in the crowd. "I just lost my... balance. That's all."

"Are you sure?" said a sweet voice. "We have a nurse," she said, grasping Albert's arm.

"Yeah, I'm sure," Albert confirmed, using the girl's leverage to steady himself. As Albert rose and raised his head, the angel stood before him at eye level. There she was, the most perfect girl he had ever laid eyes on – her hair was honey-blond, her cheeks had a rosy tone and her almond-shaped eyes radiated concern. "Thanks," he stuttered.

"He doesn't even have a scratch," said Ruth, pulling Albert in the opposite direction. "Really Albert? It's our first day and you're already embarrassing me?"

While Ruth dragged him forward, Albert struggled to catch one last glimpse of the girl who had knocked him down and helped him up. What was her name? When would he see her again? He felt transported to another time and place and a warm sensation rushed throughout his body.

Caroline Carmell was sitting by herself on a large white

chair behind a glass table shuffling though some small bright discs. Upon seeing her new students she quickly rose and moved in measured steps across the room.

"Good morning, Nicolaus. How wonderful of you to bring our new students!" said Caroline, smiling radiantly. She was a young woman, dressed smartly, with long flowing brown hair. Nicolaus had told them that Caroline was also a Chosen, but Albert wondered why his new friend hadn't mentioned how pretty she was. He wished he'd had a heads up so he could pretend he wasn't impressed. "And you, young lady, must be Ruth," Caroline gently extended her hand.

"Yes, ma'am," said Ruth, with the self-confidence that Albert had always envied.

"Please call me Ms. Carmell or just Caroline," she said, moving toward Albert. "And you are…"

"Albert. She's my… my… my… sister," said Albert as he turned to catch a quick glance of Ruth behind him.

"Oh I know all about you two," said Caroline. "But I didn't know you had a speech impediment," she said, prompting Albert to speak again. "We certainly can help you with that."

"He only stutters when he sees a pretty girl," interjected Ruth.

As Albert looked at his sister with disgust, Nicolaus broke into laughter.

"Well, thank you both very much," said Caroline as her face turned a light crimson. "But I should warn you in advance that there are many beautiful girls here throughout Gaia!"

"I have no doubt about that," said Ruth, jerking away from Albert as he tried hard to pinch her arm.

"Welcome to Gaia and to our school," said Caroline. "Each instructor is responsible for one class. With the exception of Alternative Physics with Professor Geb, you will remain in this classroom for the duration of the year. We shall begin in approximately ten minutes," said Caroline moving toward her glass desk filled with strange objects, in the center of the room. White armchairs were forming a semi-circle around her desk. "But before we do, I would like to briefly familiarize you with our subject matter, which may come as a surprise."

"Julius mentioned that we would have private lessons…" said Albert.

"He's quite right, of course," said Caroline. "It is my job to bring you up to speed. I'm preparing some additional classes for you two," she explained as she directed them to the first chairs. "Please have a seat."

The arm-chair automatically adjusted its height to the shape of their bodies and prepared its foam to not only distribute their weight properly, but to assure that they would keep an ergonomically-correct posture.

"So you all speak English here?" asked Ruth.

"Well, you will always *hear* everybody speaking English, but it doesn't mean that they are actually *talking* in English." Noticing their puzzled expressions, Caroline decided to offer further explanation. "It's just a trick that your brain plays with you. This was the way Gaia's founders found to break any communication barriers. At the moment you arrived in this planet, your brain adopted this *configuration*. That's the only alteration allowed to be performed on the Chosens."

"Interesting... but a little frightening at the same time..." said Albert. His thoughts then drifted to his father. He definitely wouldn't enjoy finding out that his brain was altered without his awareness or permission.

"Regarding our classes, we will concentrate on Physics, Chemistry, Mathematics, History of Ancient Peoples and Nutrition," continued Caroline. "Our Secret Science discussion is held once per day."

"Secret Science?" asked Albert.

"As I'm sure Julius explained, our Gaian ancestors championed the improvement and development of society. We shall investigate this in the context of dreams, symbols, vital energy and numerology," said Caroline.

"I have no idea what all that means, but I like it!" exclaimed Ruth, thrilled by the mystery of the exotic subject.

"It is voted the 'favorite subject' of the students in our elective subject elections every year," informed Caroline. "One very serious matter I would like to remind you of is the use of Intensifiers. They are strictly forbidden in my classroom."

"Intensifiers?" asked Albert.

"I can see Julius neglected to inform you," said Caroline disapprovingly. "Long range vision and hearing intensifiers have no place in this classroom. Students take these to cheat on exams. Should I discover they are being used, it is grounds for automatic expulsion."

"I got it," said Albert. "But he didn't say anything."

"They are natural stimulants with intense but transitory effects on the brain's neurons," explained Caroline. "They were developed after years of research and have no negative side-effects. They come in both chewing-gum and liquid form... But they are not to be used under any circumstances in my class."

"Long-distance hearing," repeated Ruth, dreaming of scenarios in which they might be advantageous.

"There must be other kinds too," said Albert, his imagination also running wild.

"Oh yes," said Caroline. "But now it's time to begin class."

As if on cue, several students began entering the classroom in single file. Albert and Ruth rose from their seats instinctively, standing next to Caroline while awaiting further instructions.

One by one the seats were filled, but all eyes remained

fixed on the Chosen students. Albert counted sixteen students, far fewer than he remembered from his previous school, then he simply stared at the floor to avert the watchful eyes that now encircled him.

"Good-morning everyone!" said Caroline, clapping her hands together and rubbing them anxiously. "Today, as you all know, is a very special day. Our newest Chosen students have finally joined us! As the good hosts I know you are, please welcome Albert and Ruth to the finest institution on our humble planet."

A loud applause mixed with shouts filled the air. As the twins studied each face, a cold look from one of the students sent shivers down their bodies.

"Our new primitive guests," said a girl with wavy chestnut-brown hair and round black eyes, scowling at Ruth. "I hope they were tested."

Albert felt his face burning in shame; he truly wanted to say something back, but wasn't good at quick comebacks. He tilted his head down toward the white floor, instead.

"Isadora!" shouted Caroline. "How dare you say such a thing?" Caroline fixed a reproachful eye on Isadora, who sunk back into her chair.

"Just remember that humans are animals," said Ruth defiantly. "They attack when threatened."

With that Albert raised his head and joined the other

students who erupted in convulsive laughter.

"Ruth. Isadora. Stop this nonsense immediately," scolded Caroline.

"She started it," said Ruth. "I have the right to defend myself."

"Very well. But you both heard what I said," Caroline stressed, looking back and forth to Isadora and Ruth. She then took her personal MOD from her desk and reset the configuration of the classroom. The semi-circle of arm-chairs expanded its size, giving room for two extra seats that appeared between Nicolaus and a girl in a blue dress.

"Violet and Nicolaus, you wouldn't mind having our new students sitting between the two of you, right?"

"Are you kidding me, Ms. Carmell?" said Nicolaus, lighting up the atmosphere. "It would be a great honor," he added, in a formal accent.

"My pleasure," agreed Violet. The *angel*'s voice, recognized Albert as he walked towards the empty seats.

Violet... he repeated her name in his head. As their eyes crossed again, he immediately felt his legs grow weak. The idea of spending not only the next few hours, but possibly the whole school year sitting right next to her was a little overwhelming. Before he realized it, he was frozen in front of his seat. He remained in that semi-consciousness state until a hand grabbed his jacket and pulled him down.

"You don't have to wait for my permission to sit next

to me, man!" Nicolaus chuckled, releasing his jacket.

So the worst had happened, realized Albert. The only thing he had to do was sit down next to Violet, but he couldn't handle even that. Now the only thing he could do was pretend he wasn't furiously angry at himself and come to terms with the fact that his sister would be sitting between him and... Violet. Perfect. That wouldn't be awkward at all.

"Set up your MOD," advised Nicolaus, motioning for him to copy his movements. He slid his finger to its corner and pushed down. The devise fixed itself to each armrest, forming an oval surface.

Violet guided Ruth to do the same, but something weird happened as she finished. First the device turned red, then it started to flash slowly. Suddenly, a note took over the entire screen, written in huge letters.

"Warning #1/3: Get out of Gaia! – xoxo Isadora"

"You should show this to Caroline!" Violet advised, raising her hand to call the teacher.

"That's okay," whispered Ruth, grabbing Violet's arm. "This girl wants attention and I'm not going to play her game."

"I guess you're right..." agreed Violet, leaning back in her chair.

Caroline put her MOD back on her desk and grabbed one of the scattered bright discs from her desk. She returned to the front of the classroom and before addressing the students, she threw the disc upwards. It dangled in the air for a couple second, and then transformed itself into a hologram of a boy sleeping peacefully in a bed.

"We shall now turn to the subject of Secret Science," began Caroline. "You will recall our discussion about dreams. Our Chosen guests learned of Gaia through dreams. Who would like to comment on this phenomenon?"

A thin boy with spiked black hair was the first to respond. "There are three types of dreams: Reflection, Emotional, and Revelation," he said. The three words mentioned appeared on each personal device.

"Very good, Dilson. And could you explain their differences?"

"In the Reflection, you remember things from your day, things that worry you, like taking a pop quiz," said Dilson, drawing muffled laughter from the class. "The Emotional is related to important memories of your life. Like dreaming about a dog that you used to have. The Revelation is more complicated."

"Does anyone wish to add anything? Why the Revelation-Dream is so 'complicated,' as Dilson claims?" Caroline scanned the room for volunteers. Violet raised her hand. "Yes, Violet?"

"They carry messages, or advice, things like that. They can warn you about things. But sometimes you don't know when they're happening. That's the hard part. You might think it's another kind of dream and be wrong," said Violet.

"Usually these dreams will be saved in our memory, because the process unleashes a lot of energy," added Nicolaus. "But we have to analyze the relevant message of the dream right away, to not forget it later."

"And how can we analyze a Revelation, Akil?" asked Caroline, pointing to a boy with messy blonde hair. He was slouched over his desk, with a confident grin.

"It's like this," he began. "Every detail of the dream can be the key that unlocks it. Dreams use common images as symbols."

The hologram of the sleeping-boy tossed and turned, and a white cloud formed over him, containing a blurry image of him falling down a hole.

"So what does the boy's dream tell you, Akil?" Caroline pointed to the image.

"Well... it's not like he'll fall into a hole in real-life, but the dream is telling him that something unexpected will happen and he better watch out."

"Thank you, Akil," said Caroline. "Albert, Ruth, any question so far?"

"It's an interesting subject," mumbled Albert. "But people on Earth don't seem to care about it."

"Not quite true, Albert," Caroline disagreed. "In ancient Egypt, dreams and symbols were observed and respected. There are numerous examples throughout history involving revelations through dreams. Do you know of Thomas Edison?"

The hologram boy disappeared, replaced by the figure of an aged man, with thick eyebrows and white hair, wearing a nightgown, appeared in the room. Albert immediately recognized the face from his science books. Thomas Edison seemed so alive that Albert wondered if he could purchase a device like that to get to know his own ancestors.

Thomas Edison lay down on his bed and within seconds, a cloud popped up above his head too, displaying the shape of a light bulb.

"That's how he got inspired to invent electric lighting... through a dream. The French thinker René Descartes also had a Revelation which later became the basis for modern science."

Albert listened quietly to Caroline's voice echoing around the room. These facts were all new, and he wondered why his father had never brought them up.

"Do you have a book about all of this?" Albert finally asked.

"Looks like we know more about their planet than them," Isadora sneered.

"I warned you once already young lady," said Caroline pointing an accusing finger. "You and I will have a serious talk before your lunch break." Isadora slumped down in her chair as her hostility turned to mild fear.

Albert followed closely behind Nicolaus as they made their way to the cafeteria. While they discussed Edison's mysterious dream, he kept an eye on Violet, who was walking along with Ruth right in front of them.

The cafeteria was located outside behind the immense wooden schoolhouse, and offered a spectacular view. A long and narrow lake surrounded by hundreds of shades of greens extended across the horizon.

"It's really peaceful here," Ruth admitted.

"You're right about that," said Violet, looking around at the circular tables. "But you get used to it. Where do you want to sit?"

"Don't we need trays first?" inquired Ruth. She hadn't noticed a serving area.

"The menu is on the table," said Nicolaus, smiling.

"Hey man, are you sure you're okay?" interrupted a husky voice. "That was a great entrance today!" said the guy, slapping Albert on his back.

"Yeah... I'm fine, thanks," responded Albert recognizing his face from the crowd that had gathered around him after his fall.

"And you must be Ruth. It's a pleasure to meet you. I'm Phin," he introduced himself, extending his hand to her.

"It's totally my pleasure Phin," said Ruth, shaking the hand of the boy with olive skin and gray eyes. She took a while to release his hand, and they stared at each other for long seconds. "How do you know my name already?"

"It's not common to have a Chosen at school... Sorry to say, but everyone already knows your name," Phin commented.

"So people are curious to see the new school alien?" asked Ruth.

"Exactly," said Phin, with a smile that accentuated his boyish dimples. "But, seriously, I'm glad that you decided to join us here in Gaia. I'm sure you won't regret it! And if you need someone to show you around..." A worried look fell over his face and he couldn't finish his sentence. "Sorry, excuse me."

Phin walked away, and joined a visibly enraged Isadora. After he kissed her on the cheek, Isadora gripped his arm and pulled him to her table.

"He's dating Isadora?" asked Ruth, perplexed. "You've got to be kidding. What does he see in her?"

"Isadora is one of the hottest and most popular girls at school. Don't let her attitude fool you: she can be really charming when she wants to," said Nicolaus. "But I'm sick of her tearing other people down."

Albert peeked over his shoulder, watching Isadora with Phin and their friends at the table behind them. They all seemed honored just to be sitting next to her. Nicolaus's explanation seemed plausible. Isadora had a natural beauty that shined through with her every single gesture. She was one of those girls who could captivate everybody's attention just by staying in a room. She didn't need makeup, high heels or fancy clothes. She was born looking perfect. But only on the outside. Rudeness and hostility could cancel out even her beauty and he had decided to keep a safe distance from bitter girls like her a long time ago.

As if confirming his evaluation, Ruth's MOD once again started to flash and to gravitate in front of her. She grabbed it and held it between her fingers, trying to keep the message private, but not before Albert managed to catch a glimpse:

"Warning #2/3: Go back to your disgusting planet. – xoxo, Isadora"

"Well, for sure Isadora doesn't like me and Ruth," Albert pointed out.

"She's always been like that," said Violet.

"Why?" asked Ruth.

"I honestly have no idea," responded Violet. "Let's just forget her and find some place to sit."

Their eyes scanned attentively around the crowded tables, without success.

"Seems like we were talking too long…" Nicolaus shrugs. "I guess you girls can squeeze over here…" He pointed to the nearest table. "Albert and I can sit on that table close to the edge."

Nicolaus ran to save a space on the bench, ignoring the eyes that now followed them. The awkward feeling of being watched reminded Albert of an old nightmare. For years he had woken up in panic after dreaming of showing up at school totally naked. Even knowing it was ridiculous, he glanced down to double check. Shirt, check. Pants… check. Still, he couldn't help but wonder what was going through their minds. Did they see him the same way as Isadora? As a primitive invader? The idea of being a freak on display forced him to meet their stares.

His schoolmates weren't frowning—they seemed so relaxed and incapable of showing hostility or disgust. Most of them were actually smiling and others even waved as if to introduce themselves. Albert smiled back in relief. For the first time, he was the center of attention in a *good* way. No one was throwing food at him, grabbing his underwear or putting *"pretend that I'm hot"* stickers on his back. He just hoped they wouldn't change their minds as they got to know him.

"Are you enjoying the attention?" Nicolaus asked him, with a wild grin on his face. "You know, you are almost celebrities here… Gaians love a lot of TV shows and movies from Earth, so they kind of idolize everything Earthy… One girl here was even named *Coca-Cola*! Can you believe it?"

They both laughed. "So how do we eat in this place?" he asked while sitting next to Nicolaus.

"Put your MOD on the table," said Nicolaus, rushing to demonstrate. As his personal device touched the table, photos of colorful plates popped up on the screen. "See, there's our school menu. Just touch what you want for lunch."

"Hummm… gnocchi, salad… oh… there's dessert…" chose Albert. The tabletop opened and his selected meal rose up right in front of him. Although it smelled amazing, he wasn't that interested in food… he was straining to catch a glimpse of Violet between the bodies of several dozen students blocking his view.

"You never stop looking at her," said Nicolaus, with a knowing smile.

"I'm just… trying to see the view," replied Albert sharply.

"Very funny, Albert," said Nicolaus, kicking him underneath the table. "You suck at lying. Besides, her boyfriend would kick your butt!"

This new revelation shot like a knife through Albert's chest and he jumped upright in his chair.

Nicolaus laughed so hard he nearly fell over backward in his chair. "You do like her! That look on your face proves it! I was just kidding; she doesn't have a boyfriend."

"I just want to get to know her," said Albert as the steam from his gnocchi enveloped his face. "She was the one who helped me today. I just want to say 'thanks.'"

"Yeah, and I want to move back to Earth!" Nicolaus

said holding his stomach. "Albert, you are something else."

"Yeah, something else..." Albert looked over at the faces of some of the other students engaged in conversation.

"Seriously," began Nicolaus, eating his shrimp stroganoff quickly, "I really like Violet. She's a sweet girl and one of the smartest in class."

"She looks like... an angel," Albert blurted out involuntarily.

"You could say that."

"Do you like her?" asked Albert as an uneasy feeling rose to his head.

"I love her, Albert," said Nicolaus seriously. "I'll never let another guy steal her from me." He paused. "Just kidding man, we're just good friends!"

"Good to know..." said Albert, realizing a few seconds later that he had said too much.

SIX

From the corner of the walkway, Albert could already see Ulysses standing in front of the door waiting for them. It was exciting to find out that the President lived just a few blocks away from his house, but a little disappointing too. He was expecting to see a huge mansion, surrounded by walls, security guards and watchdogs drooling with rage. Instead, Albert found himself looking at a chalet, even smaller than his former house on Earth.

"Why did the Council's president invite us for dinner?" Albert whispered to Julius, as they approached the house. "I mean, he's the president... he must be..."

"He is a very simple man and extremely friendly..." Julius cut him off. "Don't worry."

As they passed by a small triangular garden filled only with orchids, Albert caught a better look at the President. His appearance was fragile and vulnerable, with hunched shoulders and white slicked-back hair. Even so, he would never guess that Ulysses was 205 years old, as Julius confided to them.

72

"Good evening!" said Ulysses, taking a step toward the group. "It's wonderful to have you here! I must confess that I was really looking forward to meeting you; I followed your selection closely!" he said smiling. "I hope you're enjoying Gaia."

"Of course we are. It's a lovely place," offered Sarah, a little shaky with excitement.

Since Albert arrived home he had seen his mother design dozens of clothes. Her natural indecision, combined with the fear of being underdressed for dinner, made her try on a dozen options. When she finally made up her mind and settled on a long red dress, she redirected her attention to their dad. She practically forced Victor into a black tuxedo. But it didn't stop there. Albert was her next target, and had to model a dark gray suit with thin tie. He'd always hated ties, such a waste of fabric... probably Gaians didn't even use them.

Now he smiled and wondered what his mom was thinking after seeing Ulysses in plane black pants and a white T-shirt. She could have never imagined that dinner with the planet's president would be informal. So they looked like idiots. The evening couldn't have started better.

"Ulysses has been our president for more than 50 years," explained Julius, tapping the president's shoulder. "Just because he's the most evolved person, morally and intellectually, in Gaia."

"Don't believe in him!" said Ulysses. "Gaia needs a

very good looking president. And I'm a cute little old man. That's why I got the job." Ulysses signals for them to enter the house. "Please come in."

The interior decoration was as simple as the outside's. A few pieces of furniture were spread around, giving the living-room a minimalist but cozy look. The savory smell of homemade meals lingered in the air.

"Thanks for inviting us over, it's an honor to be here," said Victor.

Albert couldn't deny that he was actually having fun watching his dad try to be pleasant. First of all, he was an introvert by nature, he hated formal dinners full of people he didn't know and the superficial chatter they used to fill the silence. Secondly, Victor was still unsure about Gaia, and he claimed the dinner was just to convince them – *manipulate* was his actual expression – to stay. But the idea of investigating Gaia and their advanced technologies convinced him to accept the invite. Curiosity was stronger than his desire to avoid awkward moments.

"Please make yourselves at home." Breathing with a little difficulty, Ulysses led them to the next room.

A big wooden table was already set with bowls of soup and round dishes with colorful vegetables, rice and fish fillets. But they weren't the only ones in the room. Isadora was sitting next to Lionel, the Integration Department representative they had met back at the graffitied bench.

Albert took a step back. What was she doing here?

Ruth shot him a scolding look and he quickly got the message. They couldn't let Isadora think she had power over them.

"Let me introduce you to my family," said Ulysses. "This is Lionel, my son…"

"We already met at the Tour Center…" Lionel cut him off, standing up briefly and tilting his head in a greeting. He was dressed like his father, but with a long-sleeved blue shirt. He scrutinized the Kleins' appearance, and couldn't hide a smirk.

"Good! And this pretty girl is Isadora, my adorable granddaughter." Ulysses then turned to Albert and Ruth. "Aren't you in the same class at school?"

Albert opened his mouth to respond, but a cold answer came from the across the table. "Yeah, we study in the same class," said Isadora.

"I'm glad to hear that, I'm sure you'll all be great friends," said Ulysses, missing an ironic smile from Isadora. He took a seat and gestured for the group to do the same. "How do you like the school kids?"

"We're enjoying it a lot, we loved the lessons and subjects," confirmed Ruth.

"I just got surprised when Caroline said the date…" said Albert. "You are on year 11012? When did you start counting?"

"Our calendar started on the day our ancestors first

landed on Gaia," Ulysses said in a calm voice. "Please help yourselves," he added, starting his soup.

"And where did they come from?" asked Albert, looking around the presidential *mansion*.

The presidential mansion had no special decorations, only a few paintings. There seemed to be no fancy technology or servants. He wondered if Lionel and Isadora lived there as well. He doubted it. The house was too small for three people and probably only had one bedroom. Besides, its simple style could only belong to a selfless person, something that Isadora would never be mistaken for.

Lionel took a deep breath before explaining in a condescending tone. "They came from Atlantis, the most ancient and advanced civilization in the history of Earth."

"Are you saying that the myth of Atlantis, the legendary island, is true?" Victor scoffed, casting a doubtful eye on Sarah.

"It's not a myth just because you failed to prove its existence," snapped Isadora, slowly picking at her meal.

"For thousands of years, our civilization's knowledge of science and astronomy evolved. In time, our interstellar travels brought us to Gaia, an uninhabited planet which was correctly predicted to have the ideal conditions for a new civilization," said Ulysses.

"But why did they leave Earth in the first place?" asked Ruth, serving herself a blue juice.

"They had foreseen a series of natural disasters that would eventually throw Earth into chaos," explained Ulysses. "Sudden movements in the Earth's fragile crust caused tsunamis of unimaginable proportions submerging Atlantis for eternity."

"The Atlanteans left the planet once and for all in 9000 BC, along with all sorts of plant and animal species," added Julius.

"Why didn't the people of Atlantis migrate to another continent on Earth?" asked Sarah.

"Other societies on Earth were merely hunters and gatherers. The Atlanteans didn't want to jeopardize their natural human development," Ulysses responded.

"So, the Atlanteans decided to come to Gaia..." Albert concluded.

"They weren't in complete agreement," said Julius, reclining in thought in the wooden chair. "Some reestablished their lives in Egypt, after pledging secrecy about the history and fate of Atlantis. They could offer help with certain advanced lessons, but that was all."

"It's no coincidence that the ancient Egyptians performed complicated medical procedures, like brain surgery," said Ulysses, putting aside his soup bowl and serving himself with a small piece of fish and what looked like purple "green beans".

"Do you want to know something very interesting?"

asked Julius, looking to the twins. "Ulysses is actually a descendant of the last king of Atlantis."

"Julius!" exclaimed Lionel, rising from his chair. "How can a Council member not know the rules of his own institution? It's strictly forbidden to talk about the succession of Atlanteans with the Chosen within the 30 day period." He pounded his fist on the table and glared at Julius.

An awkward silence enveloped the room. Even Isadora seemed surprised with her father's overreaction. What was with that guy? Was he what they called *bipolar*? There was clear tension between Julius and Lionel, but Lionel's angry stare extended to Ulysses too. Was he just having a bad day, or did he really dislike his own father? Maybe having your dad as the president of a planet for decades wouldn't be that pleasant. Having an angry father could explain Isadora's attitude also. If Ulysses had been around more often with his family maybe Isadora would've had a better role model.

"Lionel, please sit down," asked Ulysses, in a soft tone. "They deserve to know more about their new planet. Besides, those rules are old-fashioned and should be reviewed. Let's see, where were we..."

"I'm very intrigued with the fact that Atlantis's scientists could forecast an event like this," said Victor. "Even nowadays scientists on Earth can't forecast Earthquakes or Tsunamis..."

"The scientists didn't forecast the tsunami," hinted Ulysses mysteriously.

"Maybe that's enough, Dad!" Lionel cut him off. "This is also a very sensitive subject."

"Don't worry, Lionel, I know my limits," said Ulysses, with a smile. "The people of Atlantis were very advanced technologically and morally. However, society was divided between those who believed in secret science and the ones who only believed in pure mathematics and rational science. Those who believed in secret science were considered deluded mystics. But one day, many 'mystics' had the same dream: Atlantis would be submerged beneath a massive tsunami."

"You're saying they were warned about the disaster by a dream?" Victor retorted, dropping his fork.

"Hundreds of 'mystics' had the same dream, which specified the date of the disaster. Atlantis's king at the time, my ancestor, was one of the rational ones and wouldn't consider leaving the island..." Ulysses paused and sipped his juice. "To his surprise, though, a few nights later he also had a Revelation and was forced to change his mind. The rest of the story you already know."

"I've got goose bumps!" said Sarah. "These stories were passed from generation to generation, I assume."

"Some of them, yes, but I have in my possession several documents detailing the story of Atlantis and the transfer of the entire population to Gaia, and also some 'magic tricks' performed by the mystics of those times. Tricks that even nowadays could bring a lot of wealth to ambitious people on Earth," said Ulysses, sharpening the Kleins' curiosity.

"These documents aren't family property," added Lionel. "But since their content requires an enlightened mind, they have to stay under presidential custody, along with other sensitive material."

"You keep these documents in your house?" asked Albert, intrigued.

"Why wouldn't I? Gaia is an extremely safe place!" said Ulysses, with pride. "We don't even have alarms in our houses!"

"And where do we Chosen fit into all of this?" asked Victor, still having a hard time digesting the whole history of Gaia.

"A simple matter of population maintenance, Gaians think they're too sophisticated to have babies," Lionel replied sharply.

"Gaia's population is too small, that's why you're selected..." added Isadora, without even glancing up at her guests.

"It is not a 'simple matter of population maintenance.' The reason is to give continuity to our existence, our dreams and goals. Not only that, your knowledge adds much to our society and evolution. Because we're so comfortable, we sometimes forget to keep innovating," Ulysses said.

"The families from Earth are carefully chosen, taking

into consideration the criteria of flexibility, morality and knowledge. Consider yourselves special people that delight us with your personal qualities," Julius proposed in a complimentary tone.

"Exactly... but those are not the only reasons you're so special," said Ulysses, wiping the corner of his mouth with a napkin.

"What do you mean?" Albert asked, puzzled.

"Albert, you never stopped to think why you were the only one who saw a red sky and had a Revelation about Gaia?" asked Ulysses.

"Of course I did..." Albert admitted.

Since his first Secret Science class, Albert had been wondering about it. What made him see things that others weren't capable of seeing?

Everyone is able to have a Revelation, but some people have a special gift for it," said Ulysses. "The tsunami dream that you had connected you with our ancestors and showed that you would be following the same path that they chose years and years ago. Your sister, Ruth, also has a gift..."

"I have a gift?" asked Ruth in disbelief.

"She has a gift? Hard to believe..." Isadora replied disparagingly.

"Yes, she has quite an interesting gift. She can bring out the joy in people. But she also brings out the truth; everybody shows their true colors when she's around. Did you notice that, Ruth?"

"Well, I've noticed that people are very honest with me..." said Ruth, facing Isadora's stare.

"But these gifts exist for a reason..." continued Ulysses. "Sarah, this may come as a surprise to you, but you're descended in small part from Atlanteans."

Another awkward silence. Albert could see his dad's reluctance to accept the direction that conversation had taken. His mom, on the other hand, seemed to enjoy putting together the pieces of this new puzzle. Albert knew she must have her own set of questions that remained unanswered throughout her life and that Ulysses's last comment must have really resonated with her.

"Wow... Now I'm really shocked..." said Sarah.

"I think we all are," offered Albert, with a half-smile.

"Including myself. Are they descendants of Atlantis? How did you hide a matter of that importance from me?" asked Lionel.

"The Council's president has the obligation to keep some important information confidential. I wanted the Klein family to be valued for their own gifts and qualities, not for their distant past," explained Ulysses.

"Sure, it was a very wise decision, Ulysses," said Julius.

"Lionel, you're acting strange today..." Ulysses grinned. "Are you ready for dessert?"

Albert tossed and turned the whole night. That was one crazy dinner. But what really stood out was that one comment from Ulysses – he had a gift. As much as he tried to keep his cool and not overthink it, it seemed almost impossible to ignore the excitement of finding out that he really was *special*... but what would it bring? How often would he have Revelations? Would his gift be something he could practice and improve? He immediately considered asking Ulysses for a private appointment to discuss his doubts, but the president certainly had more important issues to take care of. Besides, sooner or later he'd find out the answers by himself... he knew it was just a matter of time.

SEVEN

On the following morning, the Zoom left the twins at a desolate beach. Birds were singing atop the dozens of coconut palms which stood in a line beside the clear waves of the ocean, where thousands of small fish rippled the surface. Rock piers stood on both sides of the beach, where a few students were crouched, looking for mussels.

"Now *this* is what I call gym class," commented Ruth, taking a long deep breath and stretching into the morning sun.

"They require 'contact with nature,'" said Nicolaus, citing the school code. "Anyway, we're still on school property. Do you remember the view from the cafeteria?"

Ruth walked toward Nicholas with her hands on her hips. "Yeah. What about it?"

"Well, the path you saw ends right over there, near those rocks," said Nicolaus pointing in the direction from which they'd come.

Albert followed Nicolaus's finger as he slowly traced the shoreline. Just when his eyes reached the path in question, Violet's profile intervened in his line of sight. Albert reflexively staggered and fell backward. He caught his balance just in time to avoid repeating the embarrassing episode of his first day.

"Violet! I was looking for you!" said Ruth, running to meet her friend halfway.

"Good Morning!" Violet exchanged glances with them, but lingered on Albert. "How are you doing, Albert?" she asked, passing her delicate fingers through her hair.

"I'm... I'm... fine..." Albert stuttered. Dang it, he thought. Now she would think he was an idiot for sure. Why did his shyness always have to ruin his chances to be sociable and interesting?

"I was showing them where we are," said Nicolaus, saving Albert from the awkward moment. "I remember how I felt when I first..." Nicolaus's thoughts drifted away, when he looked in the opposite direction. He smiled then pointed to a short woman, around sixty years old. "Here comes Lady Rose..."

"Who?" asked Ruth.

"The principal," responded Violet, instinctively starting to walk towards the approaching figure. "Let's go. I think she's going to talk about the games."

Albert was struck with terror. How had he forgotten? He hated sports, mainly because he sucked at them. He had been so distracted by the scenery and the appearance of

Violet. But when he saw the students gathered together, he knew his ineptitude would soon be exposed. What would Violet think?

As Albert considered several ways he could fake an injury, the voice of the principal rang out across the beach.

"Good Morning, my darlings!" called Lady Rose from a platform which made her appear much taller and gave her an added air of importance. Her voice was strong and loud despite her distance from the students.

"Intensifiers," whispered Nicolaus, explaining her volume. Albert and Ruth nodded.

"Today is another marvelous day," said Lady Rose, as the students shushed each other. "We have a lot to celebrate! I've learned more dance steps to show you."

Awkwardly, Lady Rose started thrusting her hips, hopping and tiptoeing. The students encouraged her with shouting and applause.

"Everyone loves her. She's always happy and making us laugh," said Nicolaus, following up with a whistle.

"But… you know that's not why I'm here," said Lady Rose, breathless. "I'd like to announce the opening of our Olympics!"

"Oh God, really?" muttered Albert, looking up the clouds.

"Did you hear that Albert? You arrived just in time!" Nicolaus cheered.

"This year, the events will be Beach Volleyball and Swimming," Lady Rose continued. "Both as partner events. I trust you have all practiced during the brief holiday."

"Partner events?!" repeated Albert, still delirious with fear.

"Trust me, you're going to love it," Nicolaus encouraged.

"Does *everyone* have to play?" asked Albert, hoping for an escape.

"Of course everyone's going to compete, Albert," said Nicolaus. "That's the point of the Olympics. What's gotten into you? You look sick."

"Each Volleyball pair may use one Intensifier," stated Lady Rose. "Swimming pairs can add one more for breathing. You have five minutes to find your partners. Don't forget that the focus is on teamwork! Good luck to everyone!"

As Lady Rose's voice trailed off, the students frantically started looking for partners and sent in their decisions by MOD.

"What do you think of being my Volleyball partner?" asked Violet, turning to Ruth.

"Sounds great," agreed Ruth. "I love Volleyball. But I've never practiced sports using Intensifiers..."

"Think of them as vitamins," said Violet. "They only make your body respond more quickly. We just have to choose the right type."

Ruth's mind was racing as she considered some of the wilder possibilities. "I'd love to improve my reflexes, especially to defend a spike!"

"Great suggestion, Ruth!" exclaimed Violet, grabbing her MOD. "I'm going to send out our choices now."

As Violet manipulated her device, Nicolaus was still busy trying to convince Albert to return to the world of the living.

"You don't have a choice, Albert," pleaded Nicolaus, trying another angle of persuasion. "The Olympics are mandatory. Don't even try to get out of it."

"But I'll be humiliated! I really suck at playing anything that involves balls or movement!" said Albert. The last time he agreed to participate in a competition, he gained a place in the hall of shame as the worst goalkeeper in his school's history. His fame pursued him for several years.

"How do you know? You'd be a loser if you don't even try! That'd be the only way you could humiliate yourself!" snapped Nicolaus. "Besides, if you don't play you'll never improve. It's that simple."

Somehow such simple logic made sense to Albert. How could he really know? The scientific thing would be to experiment, and he had promised himself not to mess up this second chance he had to fit in. He knew he had to take risks and step outside his comfort zone if he wanted to be respected.

"Okay. I'll play," Albert conceded. "But I have to warn you, I wasn't being modest. I actually do suck."

"What about swimming?" asked Nicolaus.

"I used to swim…" Albert confessed reluctantly. "Ruth used to beat me, but she is really fast."

"Then let's swim! Now which Intensifier should we take?" Nicolaus looked at the small waves, as if asking for advice. "Maybe we just need the basic: Leg Agility"

"But won't everybody choose it?" asked Albert.

"This isn't an ordinary swimming competition," said Nicolaus. "Having balance or even more concentration can be better than just being fast." He started scrolling through his MOD quickly, ignoring the tense look on his partner's face.

"May I have your attention?" Lady Rose interrupted the mayhem. "Schedules will soon be posted. Volleyball courts are ready."

As Albert looked over his shoulder, he saw a rectangle of messy sand transform into a professional-looking volleyball court, sided by a huge bleacher.

"Caroline and Geb will be the referees," continued Lady Rose. "Oh, and one last thing: the oyster season is wonderful!"

"Oysters?" repeated Albert, puzzled. "I don't even want to know…"

"Didn't think you would… partner," said Nicolaus

smiling mischievously.

Nicolaus and Violet anxiously looked on as a large screen began to hover above the crowd, displaying the schedule of the games. As Albert took a few steps between the students to catch a better glance at the screen, he felt a cold hand grabbing his. It was Ruth, completely petrified. Albert could guess immediately why. Ruth would be playing Isadora.

Albert knew how good his sister was at sports; since they were kids she always excelled in any kind of competition. Even with a crazy girl willing to do anything to beat his sister, he was confident that Ruth would put up a good fight. Albert gave Ruth a reassuring wink, and turned to the schedules, where he learned he was just about to make his debut. He wouldn't have any extra time to get ready. Now it was his turn to freak out.

Ruth released her hand and gave Albert a tight hug. "Good luck, bro," Ruth whispered, walking backwards towards the volleyball court. After just a few steps, she ran into someone's shoulder.

"Excuse me…" said Ruth, looking up.

"Let me ask you something, where you came from, don't people watch where they go?" Phin joked.

"Very funny, Phin! I was distracted, sorry…" said Ruth.

"No need to be sorry, I wouldn't mind bumping into

you every day..." Phin blurted out, making Ruth blush instantly. "So, you'll be playing today, right?" he recovered, changing the subject.

"Yep, I guess so..." Ruth found herself short on words.

"Well, I'm sure you'll do a good job. I'll be watching!" he said, smiling.

"Phin!" A sharp voice cut the air. Isadora was just a few steps away, arms crossed, and staring angrily at them.

"Good luck, Ruth," said Phin in a low voice. "I gotta go now..."

Ruth watched Phin turn away, with reluctance and heavy steps. As he approached Isadora, the couple started to argue subtly.

"I think I've never seen Isadora so annoyed," Violet whispered to Ruth. "But it's not cool for him to look at you like that."

"Does he look at me differently?" asked Ruth, intrigued.

"You know that he does," said Violet. "I think you should be careful; you don't want another fight with Isadora."

"I was just... wondering if he knows what a poisonous snake she is..."

"Well, love is blind as they say," said Violet.

"You think they're in love?"

"Honestly, I don't know, Ruth!" responded Violet, while watching Ruth's MOD gravitate.

Although Ruth was pretty sure about the content of the message – it wasn't too hard to guess due to recent events – she grabbed the device and read the new warning out loud:

"Warning #3/3: You'll seriously regret crossing me! Don't say I didn't warn you! xoxo Isadora"

"Wow, she's going too far!" exclaimed Violet, perplexed. "You sure you don't want to tell Caroline about these messages?"

"Yeah, I'm sure, don't worry," replied Ruth. "Forget it…"

"Ruth and Violet, it's time!" called Caroline, already on the volleyball court. The teacher raised a small I-shaped bottle filled with a bluish liquid.

"So I take it those funny bottles are Intensifiers…" said Ruth, watching Caroline handing a bottle to Isadora and another to her partner Ellie, a tall, tough-looking girl.

"That's right! Let's go get ours!" said Violet, excited.

Meanwhile, Albert followed Nicolaus closely as they walked onto the rock pier, where their competition would start. The rough and sharp surface made him understand why Nicolaus had adjusted his own plastic clothes to cover each toe.

"Akil has told me his Intensifier would be Self-Control," whispered Nicolaus.

"What that's do?" asked Albert, confused.

"It makes you calmer and more focused," explained Nicolaus.

"And you're just telling me this now? We should have chosen that!" complained Albert.

"But you said you aren't a good swimmer!" Nicolaus raised his eyebrows and looked at Albert. "Akil's an amazing swimmer, but he gets nervous about the oyster search. That's how he lost our last competition."

"What kind of crazy swimming competition is this?" Albert burst out, without realizing that he had already arrived at the end of the pier alongside Geb, the gym teacher and his competitors Akil and Dilson.

"The rules are pretty simple," said Geb, who had a shaved head and looked almost young enough to be a student himself. "Each team swims to the other side of the beach and back. Whoever arrives first gets one individual point, and the first team to be reunited gets another point. If time runs out, you're disqualified."

"But don't forget that it's not about speed only," highlighted Nicolaus.

"Exactly!" agreed Geb. "There is a special type of oyster that grows on coastal rocks this time of year. Each team has to collect as many as they possibly can, but at least 10 or you're out of the competition. Whoever finds more gets 2 extra points. Got it?"

"I think so..." said Albert, not so sure. He peered into the depth. Just the pier itself was around nine feet high, and although the water was crystal clear, he just couldn't see the bottom of the ocean, just uncomfortably large fishes with strange snake-like shapes. He felt his stomach churning in response. "And I take it it's impossible to drown with the Breathing Intensifier..."

"Which reminds me that it's time for you to drink yours!" confirmed Geb, handing out the small bottles. Albert drank them each in a single gulp. The drinks were warm and sweet, tasting like a mix of berries and black tea. A slight burning sensation followed.

Nicolaus grasped Albert's arm and whispered stealthily. "The secret is: One keeps looking for oysters while the other goes back for the first point."

"Okay, I'll keep that in mind," said Albert.

While Albert tried to calm his nerves, Ruth and Violet were already on their side of the court, waiting for Caroline to start the match. From the corner of her eyes, Ruth watched Isadora and Ellie stretching up. Isadora's movements naturally attracted every guy's attention and the girl seemed to enjoy the attention but pretended to ignore it.

"She's so hideous..." Ruth thought out loud, tossing the ball from one hand to the other while walking to the service line.

Caroline whistled.

Ruth looked at the ball and then back to Isadora. What a perfect opportunity to get rid of the disgust she was feeling and also teach the girl a lesson, Ruth considered. Maybe after the game, she would think twice before sending *warnings* to her.

Ruth tossed the ball in the air and hit it hard. The ball went straight out of bounds, making Isadora laugh.

Ellie was the next to serve. Violet defended it easily, and passed to Ruth, who couldn't set straight, allowing Isadora to block the ball.

"Ruth, c'mon, get focused!" Violet whispered to Ruth amid the noise of the crowd.

Taking advantage of Ruth's apparent distraction, Ellie served the ball directly at her. This time, though, Ruth counted on the Intensifier's help. Just a brief concentration seemed to be enough to boost the liquid's effects. Before she had a clear perception of the ball's direction and speed, her arms were already pressed together and her legs carried her forward on their own accord. With no trouble, she passed the ball for Violet to set. Ruth then spiked the ball to the left corner of the court, leaving her opponents no chance. The crowd erupted in applause.

Meanwhile, Albert managed to clear his mind while he watched Nicolaus choose the best fabric for their outfits – one that would provide less friction on the water and facilitate their movements. As the clothes could assume the properties of any animal skin, Nicolaus seemed to have a hard time deciding between that of a shark or a dolphin. After a couple of minutes he set his mind on *being* a shark and adjusted his suit's length. It now covered his entire body, except his face. It tightened to form gloves around his fingers. "This is so the oysters don't hurt our hands," explained Nicolaus, handing him a bag for the oysters and setting the color of their clothes to a green and red hue. "Once you're in the water, the outfit will form a *flipper* on each foot. Come on, it's show time!"

"Okay…" mumbled Albert.

"Hey, one more thing Chosen Boy…" Geb took a thin metal from his pocket and locked it around Albert's ankle. "The Olympic Regulations stipulated as mandatory the use of this safety-mechanism. Don't even think about taking it off!"

"This anklet was designed to avoid falling accidents," Nicolaus whispered to Albert. "It can either freeze a person's movements or keep them hanging in the air. That's why I'll give you one more piece of advice – don't think too much before you jump! If you do, you will float in the air until your feelings of panic go away. I don't need to tell you that we would lose the game if this happens…"

Geb whistled. The competitors dove into the sea. Albert remained still on the pier, staring at the water. Now the fear wasn't only about the depth of the ocean but mainly related to the fact that he could chicken out while everyone was watching. Being hung in the air by an anklet would bring public embarrassment to a whole new level.

"Just jump man," advised Geb. "Do you want me to push you?"

"That would be…" Albert didn't manage to finish his sentence, as Geb ejected him forcefully into the ocean.

When his body reached the warm water, Albert started to relax. As he swam under water along with thin fish, he realized he didn't even need to go up for air. And that wasn't all. The lightness of his outfit combined with the Intensifier's effect, allowed him to slide smoothly through the waves. His legs alone propelled him, and his arms rested stretched out in front of him. Swimming was now second nature.

With almost no effort Albert soon crossed the track and arrived at the rocks on the other side, just a minute after Nicolaus and his opponents.

On the rocks, the intensifier didn't offer much help. Actually it did the opposite. With his legs moving too fast, it was hard to keep balance on that uneven ground. It took all his effort just to keep from falling, disrupting his concentration completely. The search for oysters soon became a complicated ordeal.

A loud splash noise caught his attention. He looked over his shoulders and saw Nicolaus swimming back, keeping his part of the plan. Akil dove right after, catching up with Nicolaus right at the end, arriving first.

Dilson collected oysters like a pro. His boost of "self-control" granted him incredible accuracy in his search, he didn't appear at all distracted by the mussels and other dark on the rocks. Unlike Albert.

At the same time, Ruth was growing tired and out of breath, and her serve was easily tracked by Ellie. She passed it softly back to her teammate who in turn lofted it just above the net-line for an easy spike. As Ellie's right hand descended on the floating ball, Violet's arms formed an impregnable wall, which dashed the ball onto the ground below Ellie.

Violet celebrated her move and turned to Ruth showing her red hand. "Now I know they've chosen extra strength," shared Violet.

Violet made the next two points serving the ball twice at the back corner of her opponent's court. Isadora threw up her hands in frustration.

"Really? Are you serious?" Isadora yelled at Ellie. "How come you didn't get that?"

"I couldn't..." Ellie mumbled, nervous.

"Next time I'm choosing a better partner!" Isadora cut her off. "Time out!" she ordered looking at the referee.

Caroline whistled and interrupted the game. Isadora and Ellie went to the corner of the beach to discuss their strategies privately and rehydrate with cold water.

"Isadora never asked for a time out before..." whispered Violet to Ruth, as they took a seat on the bleachers to rest, close to Caroline. "Something is telling me that she's up to something..."

"Of course she is!" said Ruth. "She wants to distract us and her strategy might work, if you're already worried."

Meanwhile, taking advantage of Albert's distraction, Dilson silently returned to swim, heading for the starting point.

The crowd of students, watching the competition from a large screen on the beach, cheered Dilson's strategy and Albert realized he'd been left behind. Albert sprang into the water, pleased to be able to rely on his intensifier's help once again. But the distance between him and Dilson was already ample, their suits and the flippers alone seemed to provide them with more than enough speed.

He thought about giving up. What was the point of keeping on trying if he wouldn't make in first anyway? What was the point of exhausting his body just to finish the competition? *Just to finish...* The thought bounced around his head. Was that the reason behind all his previous failures in life? Because he always ended up quitting? He had never managed to learn how to play an instrument because he hadn't continued the classes... he'd never learned how to play soccer because he'd felt too insecure to keep training... he'd never even won any academic competition because he'd always withdrawn his application.

Was it that hard to believe in himself and in his own

potential? Would things have been different if he had actually made an effort? A real effort? What if he actually started getting serious about winning like his opponents, instead of just coasting? What if, in spite of swimming faster than he ever had, he still wasn't giving his all? What if he tried to take advantage of his Intensifier to its maximum effect?

Albert held on to that idea and let his fears go. As his hands touched the rocks on the pier, loud applause assured him that his experiment had been a success.

"You were incredible, man!" celebrated Nicolaus, extending his hand to help Albert rise from the ocean.

"Intensifiers' are miracles, Nicolaus, that's all!" said Albert.

The scoreboard displayed one point to Nicolaus and Albert and one as well to Akil and Dilson. Trying to keep up the suspense, Geb took the bags from the competitors and started counting the oysters in full view of everyone.

"Ready for the results?" asked Geb, entertaining the small crowd. "So the total of oysters collected is… thirteen for Albert and Nicolaus and… twenty for Akil and Dilson!"

The scoreboard showed Akil and Dilson 3 vs. Albert and Nicolaus 1.

"We won!" celebrated Akil, jumping in the air and tapping Dilson's shoulder.

"Congratulations guys." Nicolaus shook his opponents' hands and addressed his partner. "Thanks for trying, Albert.

You did give it your best!"

"Thank you for making me try!" said Albert, happy to have overcome his fears.

Suddenly Geb's shrill whistle called everyone to attention once again. He walked towards Albert, his right hand clenched in a fist. "Albert, I didn't tell you anything about this because it's a pretty rare situation..." Geb started. "But, as everybody else knows, there is another way to make points in this competition..."

"You're joking, right?" Akil cut him off, in disbelief. "He didn't..."

"Yes, he did," confirmed Geb, smiling. "Albert found a pearl!" Geb unclenched his fist, revealing an opened oyster with a red pearl inside. The crowd went wild. "Congrats, Albert," continued Geb, handing the pearl to Albert. "That gives you three more points."

"So we won!" yelled Nicolaus, hugging Albert abruptly. "I can't believe it! You're the best, man!"

"That's simply... insane!" exclaimed Albert, admiring the shinning pearl.

In the mean time, Isadora had quickly returned to the court. The ironic smile had disappeared from her face, replaced by a much more focused expression. Ellie placed her hand on Isadora's shoulder and started whispering in her ears. Isadora jerked away and covered Ellie's mouth with her hand. Both stared angrily at each other, while awaiting

Violet's serve.

As Ruth had predicted, Violet was distracted enough to commit an error and the ball that she served went out of bounds.

"Violet, don't let her get to you!" advised Ruth.

Ruth deflected the Ellie's serve and passed it to Violet, who spiked it. Isadora had no problem defending and passed the ball straight to her teammate. Ellie set the ball close to the net and Isadora hit it.

A second later, a shocking scream echoed across the beach. The crowd rose, agitated. Ruth lay in the middle of the court, unconscious, with a ball-shaped mark on her face.

Violet and the students close to the court rushed to help. Isadora remained standing on the other side, showing no emotion whatsoever.

"Calm down, everyone!" ordered Caroline, blowing her whistle. "Don't move her!

"Let me take her to the school's nurse!" offered Phin immediately, and Caroline nodded in approval.

Phin approached Ruth and very carefully leaned over scoop her up. The students watched Ruth with growing concern and excitement.

"What's going on?" Albert demanded. They were planning to watch the rest of the girls' event, as theirs had already finished, but the mayhem around the court implied he was too late. He saw the figure of a girl being carried away from the beach by Phin. He didn't manage to see her face... just her hair. Her red hair. He became increasingly uneasy. He grabbed the arm of a passing boy. "What happened? Was that Ruth?"

"You missed it man!" said the student. "Isadora knocked her down! That girl didn't have a chance!"

Albert felt his entire body grow numb with anger. He could tolerate threats, but he would never tolerate physical violence against his own sister. Albert's eyes desperately scanned each student's face. When his eyes met Isadora, he sprang in her direction. He wasn't thinking straight... he wasn't sure of what to do... but he wasn't planning on letting her off easy... not this time.

When he was just a foot away, Geb stood in front of him. "Albert, calm down!"

His anger was so deep that he pushed his teacher away fiercely. Geb took a step back, regaining his balance.

"She'll be okay, Albert!" said the only voice able to cool his anger. "I promise!" Violet added. She then rushed to the bleachers to appeal to Lady Rose. "Isadora got weirdly strong after she asked for a break!" she argued. "Lady Rose, I know we shouldn't blame each other, but I really believe that Isadora overdosed."

"Well... I've never seen anything like that..." said Lady Rose, rising and going towards Caroline.

Lady Rose and Caroline whispered to each other for a

few minutes, gesturing and looking around worriedly. Afterwards, the principal called Isadora. "Please hand me your water bottle," she ordered.

"Why? You can't start blaming me for this!" said Isadora, with disgust. "Nobody here has the power to examine my belongings!"

"As the principal of this school, I have power over everything and everyone here," said Lady Rose. "Now, please, give me your bottle," Lady Rose extended her hand towards Isadora.

Reluctantly, Isadora complied. After smelling the drink, Lady Rose sipped the water. Everyone waited in silent anticipation for her reaction.

"I have no doubt that you dissolved another Strength Intensifier in your water," Lady Rose stated seriously, confronting Isadora's adamant expression.

"I didn't do anything!" complained Isadora. "I only used my first one to its full potential!"

Clearly not in the mood to argue, Lady Rose just grabbed the ball and threw it towards the ocean. The ball traveled a distance no one could have imagined, falling into the breaking waves.

"I can't believe you did that, Isadora," said Caroline with a weak, cutting voice. "No student has ever violated the dosage rules."

"Isadora, I'll have to suspend you from school temporarily, and you'll also need to report this to the Investigation Center," stated Lady Rose. "Please, tell your father that he'll need to go with you."

"I'm old enough to go to the Center by myself. Besides, you shouldn't bother... I'm sure my grandfather will take care of this issue," Isadora challenged.

Lady Rose put her arms on her waist. "You don't know your grandfather. Sit on the bench and wait for your dad," she ordered and then turned to address an apprehensive Albert. "I'm really sorry, Albert. But you don't have to worry. Our medical care is extremely effective. In a few minutes Ruth will be just fine."

EIGHT

The days passed by incredibly fast for the Klein family. Except for Victor.

During their trial period he had seemed to restrain himself from fully adapting to life on Gaia. He had avoided making friends – not talking much with neighbors, and not even accepting invitations to dinners and events. George was the only one who he had opened up to. He started waking up later and later, leaving the house only to walk the dog in the park or to attend lessons with Julius, which he didn't even pretend to be interested in. Sarah, for her part, quickly fell in love with their mystical new subjects, especially astrology and herbal medicine. Victor's reluctance to accept such "absurd theories" further divided their feelings and delayed his professional progress.

So when their thirty days were almost over, and Julius reminded everyone that it was time to decide, the decision wasn't unanimous.

Everyone in the family wanted to stay on Gaia, where they were building a life full of happiness and friendship.

Everyone, except for Victor, who no longer felt valued, appreciated or useful.

Victor finally decided he had to give in, making a sacrifice for his family's wellbeing.

Albert and Ruth were finally fitting in at school. Ruth had become quite popular after her match with Isadora. She was admired for being the only one to stand up to her, challenging her attitude of superiority that had secretly bothered so many. Isadora, on the other hand, was suspended from school for two weeks and received a warning from the Investigation Center, prohibiting her from using any type of Intensifier for one year. As the school's principal predicted, Ulysses did not excuse his granddaughter's transgression, and allowed her punishment to be applied in full.

Isadora continued to treat Ruth the exact same way, but she was careful to save her attacks for safer moments, when they were far from the eyes of Caroline and Lady Rose. Ruth started to feel sorry for Isadora, but she wouldn't let the girl's hostility get to her.

The Olympics, which were suspended after the incident, continued the following month. After the disqualification of Isadora and Ellie, Ruth and Violet wound up as champions of their sport. The final game was attended by several classes, and even though she was afraid of being a victim of yet another incident, Ruth faced her fear and played the game surprisingly well; her unpredictable moves drew loud applause. The match ended with a large advantage for Violet and Ruth as they outsmarted their opponents, who were powerless to prevent their victory.

While Ruth took a small gold trophy home, Albert and Nicolaus regretted having lost the final swimming competition to Phin and Yurk. Their competitors won by the number of oysters collected. Despite losing the final game, Albert's accomplishments became famous and he was recognized as one of the few students to have found a pearl in a competition. But Albert didn't keep his pearl; he found a better purpose for it, giving the shiny red globe as a gift. Although it made Violet blush for days, he just couldn't pass up the opportunity to show her how special she was for him. Mission accomplished.

The Olympic champions received as their prize a fancy dinner at a renowned restaurant, located in middle of the ocean, ten thousand feet below the surface. Ruth and Violet went out together with Phin and Yurk to celebrate. During dinner, while observing life at sea, Phin blurted out how upset he was about what happened between Ruth and Isadora, and apologized for not having talked to her about it before. Ruth felt even more surprised when Phin confessed that Isadora's attitude towards the competition pushed him to end their relationship, as it showed him a selfish and cruel side of her he wasn't able to accept. Violet, on the other hand, seemed to be counting down the minutes for the dinner to be over. No matter how hard she tried, she couldn't convince Yurk of her complete lack of interest in his stories about his extra athletic DNA.

One hundred and fifty days had passed since the Klein family had arrived on Gaia. One hundred and fifty days ago, Albert had been alerted through a dream about Julius, Gaia and the opportunity to change their lives completely. He had had a Revelation; a manifestation of a gift he had learned to ignore to avoid difficult questions and even feelings of responsibility. Mainly, he was just worried about having to deal with something unpredictable and so open to dubious interpretation. But he wouldn't be able to ignore his gift much longer.

"Ruth, wake up! Ruth!" said Albert, sitting on the edge of Ruth's bed, shaking her arm. "A mountain... a rough trail..." Albert thought out loud, trying to force his mind to remember the details.

"Albert, what are you doing here? I'm tired..." Ruth grumbled.

"I have to tell you about my dream!" Albert whispered. "Fog... an edge..." he murmured to himself, his head spinning around.

"Can't it wait till tomorrow?" Ruth began to slightly open her eyes.

"Darkness... winds..." He kept trying to assemble the pieces of the puzzle "It's a Revelation..."

"A Revelation?" asked Ruth, rising scared. "Are you sure?"

"Almost. I need your help to figure it out."

"The dream had hidden messages? Tell me all the details, Albert. We need to analyze the whole thing!" ordered Ruth, grabbing Albert's shoulders.

"Let's see if I can remember it all..." he started, trying to focus. "Our family was walking on a mountain path, hiking... the view was incredible... with lakes, waterfalls, wild animals... and we all seemed so happy... laughing... enjoying each moment. But the path started to narrow down and we started walking close to a dangerous edge; we had to watch our steps on this gravelly trail... then a fog came up, making things harder, and clouds covered the sky... the fog got dense and the clouds got heavier, darker... we started hearing strange voices, but we couldn't make them out... the clouds and the fog started to surround us... it was slow but intense... we could barely see each other now... we panicked and reached for each others' hand... you grasped my fist... but... we lost Mom and Dad."

"And what happened then?" asked Ruth, intrigued.

"I woke up," said Albert, nonplussed.

"Your dream creeped me out... I have goose bumps!" confessed Ruth, holding her pillow tight. "What do you think it means? We don't have enough knowledge to unravel the hidden messages..."

"I know... but there's one thing we can make out. Whatever is going to happen to us, we have to stick together, you and me. We gotta protect each other," said Albert.

"I agree… and I think it would be a good idea if we…" She stopped.

"If what?" asked Albert, curious, but she didn't respond. "Ruth? Ruth?"

"Shhhh! Can you hear that?" asked Ruth, not even moving.

"What? I can't hear anything Ruth!" replied Albert, impatiently.

Their house had amazing acoustic insulation. How could Ruth be hearing something? Maybe her ears were trained from so many years of paying attention to other people's conversation, he thought.

"Listen! It's coming from the living room," she said, slowly walking towards the door. "What time is it?"

"Around 1am…" replied Albert.

"Follow me!" whispered Ruth, leaving the room.

As the twins silently walked through the hallway, their heart sped up. There was someone in their living room for sure. More than one person, they soon guessed. But who would be barging into their place at this time of night? There was a definite tone of anger to the voices, although they still couldn't understand the words pronounced. Julius had mentioned that Gaia was a place free of criminals. Could it be he was simply wrong about that? What if he lied just to convince them to stay there in the first place? Albert went into alert mode. An advanced place like Gaia could have all sorts of weapons. How could they possibly defend themselves? They were now at the end of the hallway, shaking. Voices still unclear. Crap! The acoustic insulation was good. They had to take more risks if they wanted to protect their family. Ruth went down a few steps of the wooden staircase. Albert followed. The voices became clear.

"I'm sick of it! This is enough for me," said a familiar voice. Although they felt relieved to discover the voices belonged to their parents, they couldn't help noticing something weird was going on.

"Julius only wants what's best for our development in Gaia," Sarah replied back. "He wants the best for us, Victor!"

"The best?" snapped Victor. "First of all, he's preventing me from working! I've been studying for more than six months these same nonsense subjects. Numerology, vital energy... Why did Julius only authorize you to work? He said he has *no idea* when *I* will be ready!"

Albert could now understand what was going on. A few hours earlier, in the afternoon, Julius gave Sarah some great news. She could start working immediately. The authorization applied to Sarah only, and as much as Victor had said he was happy for his wife, they all knew it was only a matter of time before his true feelings might come out.

"I think you're upset because I'm progressing faster than you!" said Sarah.

"You believe everything people say!" Victor burst out.

"I'm an astronomer not allowed to look into a telescope! My daily tasks boils down to walking the dog in the park! Julius didn't even let me visit the Space Research Center! And how many times did he deny me access to research documents? A lot! Always with the same argument that I'm not ready yet. I may never be ready in the eyes of Julius!"

"You know that in order to have access to more knowledge you'll have to show that you deserve it!" said Sarah, on the verge of crying.

"Maybe I don't have patience for that!" exclaimed Victor. "Sarah, I miss being useful, collaborating with my peers, teaching others... What am I doing here? Gaians don't need me, my knowledge is worth nothing to them!" he said, walking towards the door.

"Where are you going, Victor?" asked Sarah, distraught.

"I don't know," he responded before leaving the house.

Sarah sprung to the stairs, sobbing, leaving almost no time for the twins to react. Tiptoeing to avoid detection, they rushed back to Ruth's bedroom.

"What was that all about?" Ruth asked Albert, carefully closing the door of her bedroom. "Do you think Dad will decide to go back to Earth?"

"I think there is a good chance..." said Albert in a breaking voice.

"But Julius was very clear about that! If we decide to

return to Earth after 30 days, our minds could be seriously damaged!" Ruth pointed out.

"I don't wanna go back and I know that you don't either," said Albert, sitting on the floor. "But we've got to be united. If our father goes back alone, it'll be the end of our family."

"Do you think this could be the meaning of your dream?" Ruth asked.

"I really hope not," Albert mumbled.

NINE

After a sleepless night, Albert and Ruth left their rooms with their stomachs growling. They ate breakfast in silence, stopping to glance at the door and the stairs, hoping their parents would eventually join them at the table. It didn't happen, though, and with their anxieties increasing, they turned to each other for reassurance.

"I was thinking…" started Ruth. "Maybe we got everything wrong… maybe this isn't the meaning of your Revelation. In your dream, we lost Mom and Dad in the darkness, but only Dad is angry with this situation… Mom didn't leave home, she didn't disappear – she's right here!"

"You don't get it… the darkness is metaphorical…" said Albert. "Whatever affects Dad, will affect Mom. She's still crying since Dad left! Do you think she'd be the same person if he disappears? No, she'd be crushed. If we lose one on them, we end up losing both."

"I'm so nervous!" Ruth confessed.

"Don't be. Mom needs us now," said Albert. "Ruth, yesterday when I told you about my dream, you mentioned something about a good idea, but you didn't finish your sentence... What were you going to say before you heard the voices?"

"Well, I was going to say that we shouldn't mention your dream to Mom and Dad. We should keep it to ourselves," said Ruth.

"I totally agree," replied Albert.

"And I also think we need some help to decipher your Revelation. An impartial opinion," continued Ruth.

"We could ask Caroline for help… She's almost an expert on this stuff and I'm sure she'd keep our secret."

"You're right…" agreed Ruth. "But we don't have class today… I can't wait almost two days to talk to her. I'm too nervous for waiting!"

"We could call her," Albert suggested. "I don't think she'd mind."

Caroline's messy hair, creased face and heavy-lidded eyes gave away that she'd been fast asleep. Embarrassed, Albert apologized and offered to call her later, but Caroline insisted on hearing about the dream. Albert slowly narrated it, but she gave no response. Not until she poured herself some coffee with no sugar and made him repeat everything from the beginning.

"Well, obviously your Revelation refers to your family. Let's try to analyze it," Caroline commented, in a collected voice. "Heavy clouds like that symbolize the arrival of an event of great intensity, and the darkness that covered you shows that the event will occur suddenly, making you feel lost."

"We couldn't see anything in the darkness, except..." Albert pointed to Ruth. "Except for each other."

"That's the worst kind of darkness, and it means that you'll feel temporarily blind," Caroline added. "And you were close to an edge. A high and deep edge I assume, since you were on a mountain. So the darkness could end up leading you to a terrible fate."

"Wow, it gets worse and worse..." complained Ruth, apprehensively.

"But you have the chance to change the situation, by uniting together to dispel the darkness," said Caroline.

The twins took a deep breath, to absorb everything that was said.

"Thanks a lot, Caroline," said Albert. "Sorry to bother you with this."

"If you need any help, you know where to find me," offered Caroline. "I'll be hoping that your intuition guides you, and that you'll have the knowledge to deal with this situation. And can I give you a little friendly advice?"

"Sure, we'd love that," replied Ruth.

"Take care of you mom. She needs to know that she can count on you," Caroline suggested.

"You're right. We'll do that," said Albert. "Thanks

again."

They turned off the device, returned the dirty dishes back to the cupboard for cleaning and, following Caroline's advice, they went upstairs to check on Sarah.

The door was half open. Sarah was lying in bed with swollen, reddish eyes, mechanically petting Soap. She didn't even notice their presence. Albert had never seen his mother like that before; she always seemed to have an inexhaustible source of cheerful energy.

Albert entered the room. His mother didn't return eye contact. He sat down next to her and held her hand. Ruth followed.

"Mom," Albert began. "We overheard you and Dad arguing last night…"

"Don't be so sad, Mom…" said Ruth, wiping a tear on Sarah's face. "He's just missing work. Soon he's going to find out how wrong he was and come back home."

"I don't know about that…" Sarah whimpered. Her eyes fixed on a bird perched on a branch just outside the window. "When your father is upset, he regrets it a few minutes later. But for the first time ever, he didn't even come back home! He's never done that to me! He never stayed a whole night away from home!"

"He's probably trying to calm down before he comes back," said Albert. "He loves you and would never do anything to hurt you."

"Well, he hurt me a lot with his attitude. It's already morning and there's no sign of him!" She began to cry inconsolably.

"Did you try to reach him?" asked Ruth.

"He left his MOD here," Sarah responded.

"Maybe he's with George," Albert suggested. "Did you call him?"

"I'm too embarrassed to call a friend and ask about my own husband. If he wanted to come home he'd be here already," complained Sarah in frustration. As she finished her sentence, her MOD grew red and began to float in front her.

"See, it's him!" shouted Albert, relieved. "No reason to worry!"

"It's not, him," stated Sarah, grabbing her device. "It's a message from Julius. He is asking me to meet him at the Council."

"Do you think Dad went to talk to him about returning to Earth?" asked Ruth.

"I don't know sweetie. Maybe..." Sarah said, robotically rising from her bad.

The Council headquarters had the form of a giant golden pyramid. The building was far the highest one that Albert had seen in Gaia and it glowed so intensely under the sun that his eyes squinted in protest. It was surrounded by nothing but yellow and green pruned trees, placed in ascending order, flower beds organized by color, and several small lakes.

Julius was leaning against the sloping wall, next to an emerald green door, devoting all his attention to his personal device. Victor wasn't with him – an indication that something was off, thought Albert.

The sound of their steps on the glass pathway alerted Julius and he slowly straightened up and stared in their direction.

"Hello Julius," said Sarah, shaking Julius's hand. "The kids wanted to come with me. I hope it's not a problem."

"Not at all," he replied. "I figured you would come together."

"This place is amazing!" Albert exclaimed. "I take it it's not a coincidence that it looks like the Egyptian pyramids..."

"The pyramids have always been the symbol of the Council's headquarters, since the time of Atlantis," explained Julius.

Albert frowned. Julius was way too succinct in his explanation. He always seemed to be waiting for some cue to start a monologue about Gaia's history, but this time he didn't even offer a second sentence.

"How is Victor?" Sarah cut him off. "Can we see him?"

"Before you see him, I'd like to explain what happened..." said Julius.

Albert now was sure that something serious had actually occurred. He held his mother's cool hand in an attempt to calm her down.

"Please tell us what's going on," asked Sarah.

Julius cleared his throat. "Victor was found this morning by a pedestrian. He was on the street, unconscious."

Albert's hand supported his mom's swaying body.

"On the street?" repeated Albert.

"He was lying on the sidewalk, completely blacked out," continued Julius. "The person who found him unsuccessfully tried CPR; then she called Gaia's emergency service."

"Did they reach him in time?" asked Ruth. "Did he wake up?"

"Yes, he was taken immediately to the hospital and is feeling better," said Julius.

"That's a relief..." Sarah restarted to breath.

"Unfortunately the bad news doesn't stop there. Do you want to sit down?"

"No, Julius, we're OK," answered Albert, quickly. He hated when people had important news but started beating around the bush.

"Victor was found on the sidewalk in front of Ulysses' house," Julius informed. "The door of the house was wide open, which was highly unusual; it caught the emergency workers' attention."

"What are you trying to say, Julius?" asked Sarah, still trembling.

"There was a burglary last night at Ulysses' house," Julius began. "The intention of the robber was to steal all of the confidential information and knowledge that was under Ulysses' custody. Victor and George are the main suspects. George was also found unconscious, next to Victor, and both of them had in their possession old papers and manuscripts. They also had Ulysses' MOD, which was full of confidential information."

"You're saying they're thieves?" asked Sarah, placing her hands on her cheeks.

"They would never do that!" exclaimed Ruth.

"There must be some mistake," added Albert, looking desperately at Julius, as if demanding some more reasonable explanation.

"Sorry to be the bearer of this sad news. Victor and George will have to stay at the Investigation Center for a while," informed Julius. "The Center's office is located beneath the Council." He pointed to an outside elevator. "I'll take you to see them."

The Investigation Center looked like a huge office, with transparent tables and white chairs. The walls had the same material as an MOD and were filled with maps of

Gaia and photos. Albert's eyes lingered on one in particular. It showed his dad, unconscious, lying on the ground, surrounded by several documents. He looked... lifeless... dead. Just seeing the picture left him deeply disturbed and motionless. His family meant everything to him. Everything. He couldn't bear the idea of losing a loved one like that... so suddenly. Despite all he heard that day, his dad was still alive. And that was what really mattered.

After passing several tables, where the officials did not interrupt their work even to look up, the group stopped in front of a huge green wall, with a gelatinous texture. Julius took out his MOD and put it against the wall. The obstruction disappeared, giving way to a clear room with a sofa.

Sophia was sitting with her hands on her head, when she saw them entering the room. Nicolaus was by her side, hair completely disheveled, wearing shorts and flip flops – maybe it was his way to protest for being dragged to the Council without further explanations, considered Albert.

"Do you know what happened already?" asked Sophia, walking towards Sarah.

"Yes, we know everything, Sophia," said Sarah, holding her friends hands. "I'm sorry that George was also involved in this matter. I hope that they have a reasonable explanation for all this."

"I hope so. I can't stand this anguish of not talking to my husband!" Sophia complained.

"You can talk to them now. They are in the other

room." Julius pointed to another gelatinous door, on which he used his MOD one more time.

Victor and George were in a large room, which contained two sofas, a cabinet and a door to a small bathroom. Although Albert was expecting a terrifying environment similar to that of a prison cell, the atmosphere of the place seemed peaceful. It was decorated with bright colors, several vases of flowers and had a transparent wall, providing a beautiful view of the park next door.

Victor was sitting on the sofa facing the view, while George was lying on the other. When they realized the presence of their visitors, the two men stood up and flung their arms out to embrace their family.

"Sarah, I'm so sorry for the way that I talked to you, yesterday. I don't know why I acted like that." Victor hugged his wife passionately. Sarah couldn't hold her emotions in and began to cry.

"Please tell us it's not true," begged Albert.

Julius coughed. "Victor, I brought them up here because I think you owe them an explanation."

Albert couldn't help noticing the frighteningly sharp look that Julius cast to his father. He felt his body freeze. There was something else that Julius hadn't told them... something darker... Victor seemed confused and ashamed... lost in thoughts.

"First I want to tell you that I love you very much. I

never wanted to see you suffering like this," began Victor, in a sad tone. "Last night I had this strange, angry, impatient feeling. After I left home, I called George to talk. Unfortunately, George couldn't calm me down, because he was frustrated too. He'd been scolded at work for wanting to know more than he was allowed to."

"So you decided stealing would make you feel better?" asked Sarah, disappointed.

"No!" exclaimed Victor.

"No?" asked Ruth, trying to understand.

"Actually, I don't know!" Victor replied, holding his own neck. He tried to control his quick breathing for a few seconds and then locked Sarah's hands between his. "I just don't remember anything else! That was my last memory of the day."

"And to top it off, my memory is blank too," added George. "It's as if my night ended with our conversation. After that I just remember waking up at the hospital..."

"They're telling the truth," said Julius. "Our investigators examined their memories. A huge gap was noted. It's as if their recent memory had been deleted."

"So they must be innocent!" opined Sophia. "I mean, if they had actually committed the robbery, they would remember every detail!"

"Not exactly," replied Julius. "We believe Ulysses put some sort of chemical defense in his secret documents, which, when in contact with a stranger's skin, could make the person unconscious for hours."

"Ulysses wasn't at home then?" concluded Sarah. "Why don't you ask him about this?"

"Sarah..." Victor stared at his wife's teary eyes. "Ulysses is… dead," he mumbled.

TEN

"**U**lysses had a heart attack during the robbery," Julius informed them solemnly. "Probably due to the shock of seeing his home invaded."

"I can't think straight..." said Sophia, leaning against the wall. "Ulysses... dead?"

"I'm shocked," declared Sarah, sitting beside Nicolaus. "So you're not only being accused of theft, but also of provoking the president's death?"

"Julius, you do believe in their innocence, don't you?" asked Ruth. Her voice tone was inquisitive, but friendly at the same time.

"I know these two men very well and the purity of their hearts," said Julius. "But at the same time, all of the evidence suggests that they're guilty. Their last examined memories show a motive..."

Albert immediately recollected his parents' discussion that night. Certainly that was what Julius referred as a motive. In fact, his dad's words and attitude could put him in serious trouble. He had made some pretty offensive comments about Julius and how fed up he was with the tutoring process. Albert wondered how it must had been hard for Julius to hear all that when Victor's memories were being analyzed.

"Besides, we haven't had a serious crime in Gaia for centuries..." Julius continued.

"You mean that because we came here, we're the main suspects?" asked Sophia, staring indignantly at Julius.

"It's not that Sophia, we just don't have any other suspects," stated Julius. "We don't have reports about anyone else who wanted access to Ulysses's confidential documents. On top of that, Victor was aware that Ulysses kept confidential documents at his home and also knew about the absence of alarms at his residence, as Ulysses told him during dinner the other night."

"Julius, it seems like you're against them!" exclaimed Sophia.

"I'm not against anyone, Sophia. I'm deeply hurt by what happened as well!" said Julius.

"Go easy on him, he's feeling overwhelmed too," George intervened. "There's nothing that proves our innocence."

"Exactly," interrupted a strange voice, barging into the room. "The investigators are examining all of the relevant facts. Their judgment will be announced in two weeks."

"I'm sorry, but you are..." asked Sarah to the stranger.

"I'm Randy Vurk," said the short sturdy man, his triangular face framed by a goatee. "The Chief Investigator. Visiting time is over."

"Could you give us a few more minutes?" asked Julius.

"Julius, you didn't even have authorization to bring visitors. Escort them out now, before you break any more rules," Randy ordered.

Albert could hear Julius's exasperation.

"They didn't have a chance to say good-bye to each other yet..." protested Julius.

"That's okay," said Sarah intervening. "We had enough time. Thanks Julius, for bringing us here in the first place."

"Please leave now, then." With an open palm, Randy showed them the exit. "I have a few questions for our suspects here, if you don't mind."

Albert obeyed the order, but then returned to his father's side and hugged him strongly.

"Don't worry... I'll take care of them."

"I know you will, son," said Victor, not able to hold back a few tears coming.

Albert patted his dad on the shoulder and, before the Chief Investigator could lose the rest of his patience, he exited the room.

"Sorry about that," Julius apologized, while the wall reemerged behind him. "Randy is very strict..."

"We understand…" interrupted Sarah. "There are a few things I'd like to discuss with you if possible."

"Well, we can go to my office," offered Julius. "Although I can only allow visitors older than twenty…"

"That's okay, you can talk in privacy. The three of us can find our way out," said Albert, turning to give a quick hug to his mom. "We'll wait for you outside."

Albert's hands were still shaking… from the anger of seeing his Dad being held like a dangerous person, for the way his family was torn apart, for loosing so fast the opportunity of being happy and fulfilled in a place he was chosen to be part of. But there was something else… he was mad at himself… for questioning his father's innocence… he knew it was a crazy thought… above all, Victor Klein was a good person, with a good heart… but lately his father had changed so much… he had become bitter and defensive. Albert shook his head in disbelief. His Dad wasn't a criminal. He just wasn't.

"Look out!"

Before Albert could prevent it, Nicolaus was already hitting the floor, bringing someone else down with him.

"Are you okay, man?" asked Albert, bending over to help his friend.

"I guess…" said Nicolaus, holding his knee.

"At least this time it wasn't me who stumbled!" joked Albert.

As he lifted his friend, he looked to his side and saw Ruth helping the victim of Nicolaus's carelessness to grab his belongings on the floor.

"You really needed to be standing right next to the elevator?" grumbled Lionel, picking up his suitcase that had fallen open. Nicolaus didn't respond, but just stared at the floor. "You're the last people I wanted to see today!"

"Intensifier?" asked Ruth, handing a small bottle back to Lionel.

"Give me that now!" snapped Lionel. "Without intensifying my patience, I'd be trying to make your father suffer as much as I am!" he said, before taking a deep breath. "I guess I'll need more than one bottle."

"I'm very sorry for your loss, but I guarantee my dad is innocent," offered Ruth.

"Guarantee? You should learn to respect the feelings of victims, instead of defending murderers," Lionel burst out, turning his back on them and walking away.

The afternoon was a blur. Albert, Ruth and Sarah returned home in silence, and remained quiet for several hours, as if the silence could fill the void in their hearts. It only increased their anxiety, though. Albert desperately wanted to know what Julius had told their mom in the office, but he didn't want to pressure her to say anything. The moment she would start speaking, her weak voice would give her away.

"Mom..." Albert started as they were all seated on the sofa. "Don't hide anything from us... we're stronger than you think, and we want to take care of you as much as you take care of us... let us help... just give us some credit, please."

"Oh dear, that's so sweet," said Sarah, with teary eyes. "Sometimes I forget how grownup you are, and how you wound up to be so mature. I'm very blessed to have such incredible kids in my life..." She kissed Albert and Ruth on their foreheads. "You're right, son. There's no reason to keep secrets from you... we need to resolve this together."

"That's right, Mom," Albert comforted her. "Please tell us what Julius told you. What will happen if they are found guilty?"

"Well... Julius said that they'll probably be held prisoner for twenty years or more," shared Sarah.

"No chance of simply sending us back to Earth?" asked Ruth, perplexed.

"He said that that might be suggested, especially by those who don't support the immigration system..." said Sarah. "But other people would say that a return to Earth would be more of a gift than a punishment... since they wouldn't even remember what happened."

Albert analyzed the options. His father in prison. His mother depressed. Their family broken inside, living in shadows. A constant state of embarrassment. Yes, if he got to choose, he would decide to go back to Earth and keep his family together. Although that would imply going back to his mediocre life, with no friends, no "special gift" and... no Violet.

"And what does Julius think?" asked Albert.

Sarah looked a way for a second, gathering the courage to speak. "If we return to Earth now, our memories will be seriously damaged. We could develop deep amnesia and even brain injuries... Julius doesn't think that would be fair to any of us..."

"And... who will decide on that?" asked Ruth.

"Because they're not Gaians, if the Council declares them guilty, then their destiny will be voted on by the population..." said Sarah, distraught.

"By the population? Everybody loved Ulysses... they wouldn't go easy on them..." reflected Albert. "By the way, do you think the news has already spread around Gaia?"

"There's only one way to be sure... let's watch the news," suggested Sarah, expanding her MOD. It grew until it covered multiple walls and the images appeared in 360 degrees all around them.

"Ulysses's death moved the entire population, and the pain is felt everywhere..." said the reporter, as they started showing images of all buildings and houses projecting Ulysses's face, children and their parents crying, and teenagers leaving school in shock. "Protests demanding imprisonment and also the deportation of the accused are already taking place," continued the reporter, as the channel showed dozens of people in front of the Council. The *camera* zoomed up on shirts with caricatures of Victor and George behind bars or flying back to Earth. The images projected by the device were so real that the Albert felt as though he was actually facing all those people. He couldn't help but feel vulnerable and terrified.

"That's enough," said Sarah, turning off the channel and resizing her device.

"Look at this…" gasped Albert, glancing over his shoulder towards the entrance of their house. Through the transparent walls, they could see a crowd starting to gather on their lawn, also wearing clothes covered in outraged messages: *"Justice Now," "Go Back to Earth," "We trusted you," "You don't belong here,"* etc.

Ruth and Sarah started pacing backwards, as if the house would be invaded at any second. All the flowers in the pots started to exhale the calming scent of lavender. They had been programmed to help calm those inside when extreme levels of stress were detected, but that seemed ridiculously unhelpful at a time like this.

Albert tried to think fast and adjusted the wall's appearance to brick inside and out.

"I'm glad I locked the doors today…" said Sarah. "I'm going to prepare something for us to eat…"

As Sarah walked towards the dining room, Ruth's MOD turned green and floated in front of her.

"It's a message from Violet…" said Ruth.

Violet… the name capable of freezing his whole body. He wondered what she already knew and what her opinion about that craziness was. She didn't get to know his parents much, so she would have no reason to doubt the investigation's rumors. He just hopped that she wouldn't begin to avoid his company and grow apart… he wasn't ready to let her go just yet.

"What did she say?" asked Albert, afraid to know what the answer would be.

"She's just saying that she's on our side no matter what happens. What about yours? What does it say?"

Albert was so distracted that hadn't even noticed that his device was floating in front of him as well. He grabbed it and read the message out loud. "I hope you're okay. I'm sure this is just a big misunderstanding. Please let me know if you need anything. Sincerely, Caroline."

They still had friends who supported them. He wasn't expecting that. It made his whole body feel lighter and his mind feel clearer as if taking a huge weight out off his shoulders.

"What the heck…" complained Ruth, watching her MOD turn red, highlighting the urgent content of the message, and expand by itself. An emblem of an opulent dragon spitting fire filled the entire screen. The picture faded into Isadora's face.

"You've had your warnings that you don't belong in Gaia," said Isadora. "We don't welcome thieves and murderers. We're superior beings and your presence must be eliminated before it causes more problems."

The device shrank, leaving Albert and Ruth dumbfounded.

"Who were you talking to?" asked Sarah, from the dining room.

"No one," responded Ruth. "No one important."

"Good, because we have guests now..." informed Sarah, returning to the room, followed by Sophia and Nicolaus. "The only entrance that I authorized on our Zoom today," she said, trying to show a simile. "You came just in time for dinner."

"I'm too stressed out to eat now, Sarah..." said Sophia. "Apparently no one is concerned about looking around for evidence; they're acting like they're sure about Victor and George's guilt."

"What do you mean? They should be doing a full investigation of Ulysses's house!" Sarah exclaimed.

"But they aren't," said Sophia. "I've been staying in front of the house all day, disguised. When Randy, the investigator, approached the house I asked if they were collecting more evidence. Do you know what he said to me?"

"Just tell them, Mom..." said Nicolaus, cheerlessly.

"He said that all potential evidence was found next to

the suspects after the crime! He went there only to lock up Ulysses's house," said Sophia, pacing back and forth.

"We need to tell this to Julius!" suggested Albert, rising from the sofa. As a member of the Council, Julius had connections and could order someone to begin a serious investigation or even volunteer to double check the evidences by himself.

"Julius knows," said Sophia. "Didn't you notice that yesterday he didn't express the slightest interest in even considering other suspects? He's too mad or too disappointed to help them..."

"But if they don't look for clues, the investigation will be over soon, and our dads won't have a chance!" Ruth despaired.

"Exactly," Sophia agreed. "If we don't do anything their fate is sealed... Sarah, late tonight we've got to go to Ulysses' house to look around..."

"I told her that's a crazy idea," Nicolaus interjected.

"With Gaian make-up no one will recognize us..." said Sophia.

"Nicolaus is right, this is nonsense!" agreed Albert.

"All of the Zoom entrances are digitally controlled and were made by the same company..." continued Sophia. "I hacked that company's system and got a master-password that'll allow us access to Ulysses's garage..."

"Okay. I'll go with you," stated Sarah.

Albert winced.

"What?" exclaimed Ruth.

"No, Mom! You can't go!" said Albert, desperately. He couldn't stand the thought of losing another parent. What was she thinking? How could she dare to risk so much?

"It's our only chance!" said Sarah. "Kids, I can't stay here just waiting for a solution! I can't abandon your dad to his own fate... This is the least I can do... I need to help him. If another person committed the crime, we might end up finding something over there."

Albert took a deep breath. He knew she had already made her decision. Sarah had a huge heart and would never hesitate to put herself in danger for her family's sake. There was nothing he could do to change her mind.

"So I'm going with you," said Albert.

"No. You'll stay here, Albert," Sarah stated. "I'm going to take care of this with Sophia, alone. I promise that we'll be careful and come right back. But I need to know that no matter what happens to us tonight... you will all be here... safe."

"Nothing bad is going to happen, I have the perfect plan," Sophia assured them.

"Okay. Do what you have to do, then," said Albert.

ELEVEN

Soap's whining went off like an alarm clock. Drowsily, Albert patted the dog, trying to shut him up, but it became more and more shrill. He opened his eyes slightly. Ruth was sleeping by his side, and Nicolaus on the floor, with his MOD floating right above his head. Albert prodded Nicolaus, with some help from Soap, who licked the boy's face.

"Hey…" mumbled Nicolaus. "Let me sleep, dog…"

"Get up guys, I think we have news," said Albert rubbing his eyes.

"What kind of news?" Ruth dragged her body off the sofa.

"I don't know, Nicolaus's device is red," Albert pointed.

"Red?" Nicolaus jumped from the floor. "Let me check…" he said, grabbing his MOD. "Weird…"

"What happened? What is it saying?" Albert questioned.

139

"It's from my Mom… she's asking us to meet them right now at the IC," informed Nicolaus.

The twins and their friend looked at each other in silence, hoping for the best while trying to prepare themselves for even more bad news.

They arrived by Zoom at the Council's main entrance shortly before 5am. The sun was rising, timidly illuminating the pyramid and its surrounding park. There was no sign of Sarah, Sophia or any protestors.

"Do you think they're on their way?" asked Albert, his eyes scanned the area.

"I don't think so," replied Nicolaus. "They should have arrived here by the time they sent the message."

"The Council is probably closed, it's too early…" said Ruth, impatiently.

"Let's check and find out then," suggested Albert, adrenaline pumping through his veins.

"Isn't it too risky? If someone sees us, they'll think that we are up to something," Nicolaus opined.

"The worst thing that can happen is that we'll have to explain that we have new evidence for the investigation," said Ruth.

"Okay. Let's go inside, then," Albert decided, pacing towards the elevator.

After checking around one more time, Albert stepped into the circular mark on the floor, with Ruth and Nicolaus following behind. Within a split second, they were on the floor of the IC. The lights were on, and although the investigators desks were empty, the office wasn't closed.

Albert saw his mom standing at the corner of the room and his face lit up. She was still disguised—her skin was darkly tanned, and black curls fell across her face. Sophia stood next to her, looking like an old Japanese woman. But they were not alone. Julius, Lionel, and Randy were behind them, alongside a short old man, with black-dyed hair. Something was wrong with that picture... he just didn't have a good feeling about it.

When the elderly man saw them, he gestured for them to come closer.

"Hello. I'm Milet, the new Council President," the man introduced himself, his puffy dark eyes denouncing fatigue. "I'm here to decide about the new developments that occurred tonight. Randy and Lionel called me here to resolve this with you."

"Are you going to release my Dad?" asked Ruth.

"Don't play dumb," snapped Lionel.

"Unfortunately it's not a matter of releasing your fathers, but to decide who you'll be living with, until the judgment date," Milet continued.

"What are you talking about?" asked Albert, his mind racing.

"We just arrested your mothers for breaking into Ulysses's home," began Randy, looking down on Albert. "They're being held as your fathers' accomplices and intended to collect the rest of the secret data that remained in the house."

"But you're wrong!" Nicolaus objected. "They were only up there looking for clues that could prove our dads' innocence!"

"We already told them that," said Sophia. "They don't believe us..."

"You disobeyed Gaia's law by invading a place that was sealed for investigation," Randy accused. "You didn't even tell us about your plan. It's clear that your intention was to break our rules."

Albert glanced at Julius, hoping for some backup. But he wouldn't even look back. Just a few months ago he had sworn to take care of them at Gaia and now he would simply turn his back away? Did he really think his Dad was guilty or he just didn't want to dirty his hand?

"If we had said something about our plan, you'd have had us arrested immediately!" Sophia said in her defense.

"You should have trusted our investigation," Randy counterattacked. "It looks like you were only finishing what your husband's began."

"Until your parent's trial, we must find a place where you, kids, can be safe and well cared for." Milet turned to the group.

"The thing is that nobody wants to be with you," Lionel lashed out.

"This isn't true," Julius intervened. "I'd like to have your custody. But as a Council member, I'm not allowed to do so. Taking care of you would interfere with my obligation to be impartial at the trial. I'm sorry."

Of course you wouldn't do that, Albert mused bitterly. Why would you risk your own reputation with defending the useless family of some Chosen criminals?

"So, I suggest that we create a room here at the IC for them," said Lionel.

"They can't stay at the IC, since they aren't being accused of anything," Milet objected.

"I believe I have a solution for this matter," said Julius. "I just need a few minutes to contact a person I trust."

Albert wanted to refuse his help with an assertive denial. Bur unfortunately it seemed they had no other options.

"In the meantime, can we talk to our kids?" Sarah addressed Milet.

"Sure," agreed Milet. "Julius, please take them to a private room."

Julius sighed and led the way through a corridor, stopping at the first door to his right. Wordlessly, he opened the door with his MOD and extended an open hand for them to enter, before leaving abruptly.

"Can you please tell us what happened?" asked Ruth.

"When we were investigating, Randy caught us by surprise," began Sophia. "He had installed a body-heat detection system that recognizes the human form. As we passed by the garage, the system alerted him."

"Please forgive us, kids," said Sarah as she held Albert and Ruth's hands. "We didn't want to leave you in this situation. But at least we had enough time to search for evidence."

"Did you find something?" asked Nicolaus.

"With the help of a laser flashlight that detects footprints we found signs of four different people in the living room in the last 48 hours," Sophia shared. "In Ulysses's bedroom, the place where all the secret information was located, we only found traces of two different footprints: one was barefoot and the other wasn't."

"Obviously the barefoot prints were from Ulysses, who'd been asleep, but whose footprints were in his bedroom?" Sarah questioned.

"And whose footprints were in the living room?" asked Sophia. "One set was from Ulysses and the others were from Victor and George. But whose are the other footprints? It proves our theory: someone is behind this crime and wants to frame Victor and George."

A calm piano music started playing, detecting their disturbed mood.

"How do we know the footprints weren't made by investigators?" snapped Albert.

"Because their type of job requires the use of special shoes, which don't leave any mark or trace at a crime scene," Sophia explained.

"Did you tell the investigators?" Ruth inquired.

"Yes, but they don't trust us," said Sarah.

"Unbelievable!" Nicolaus complained. "They didn't even want to check out what you'd found?"

"The Investigation Center is closed, it doesn't open for a few more hours. And to send an investigator they'd have to go through a lot of bureaucracy," said Sophia. "The problem is that the laser flashlight is only able to detect footprints left in the last 48 hours. That time ends at six o'clock in the morning."

"So by the time someone arrives at the house, they'll only notice our footsteps and Randy's," concluded Sarah. "Kids, we're only telling this to you because we don't want you to think that Victor and George are guilty. Someone is behind all this, but please don't make the same mistake we did. Don't try to investigate by yourselves. We don't want to see them arrest you too. Please behave yourselves," she begged.

The sound of someone knocking put an end to their conversation.

Milet opened the door slightly, entering the room with cautious steps.

"I think we have the solution to your custody case," said Milet, with a gentle smile. "Julius, please bring your friend up here," he called, turning his back, his voiced echoing through the corridor.

Julius obeyed the order and appeared in the room, accompanied by a young woman.

"You don't have to do that…" began Albert, looking at the familiar face. "Are you sure?"

"My pleasure to help," said Caroline, approaching the group. "I hope you don't mind staying with me for a while."

"It'll be a little weird to live at my teacher's house," said Nicolaus. "But I'm glad you're helping us."

"Thanks, Caroline, we're honored by your gesture of solidarity." Sarah hugged Caroline.

"You don't need to thank me," said Caroline, affectionately. "Don't worry; I'll do my best to take care of your kids."

Caroline lived by herself, in a house near the school. The place was decorated with bold colors – a purple sofa, bright orange ceiling and red gadgets spread around. The living room smelled like a mixture of vanilla and peach. Two entire walls were decorated with memory videos, half of them of when she was a baby, along with her parents. The other half showed her at different ages, playing sports, dancing, and smiling… but her mother wasn't appearing in any of those... only her dad. Albert looked at Caroline with sympathy.

After a quick tour of all the rooms, she prepared a huge breakfast meal for her new guests. Sandwiches, eggs, cake, yogurt, and juices were perfectly organized on a green tablecloth.

Albert was trying hard to smile. The last thing he wanted was to look ungrateful, but he was still having problems digesting the recent turn of events. He was a mess inside, feeling alone and abandoned. His life was upside down, crashed, and although he knew he had to do something, he just couldn't find the strength to react.

"Isn't this house too big for you?" Nicolaus broke the silence, while ferociously devouring a sandwich.

There was no sign of concern on Nicolaus's face. How did he manage to be so calm? Albert questioned himself. Probably nothing had actually yet sunk into Nicolaus's mind... or maybe his friend was just an eternal optimist who never gave up hope... he secretly wished he was a little more like that as well.

"Yes, it is... It felt bigger after my Dad passed away... but soon my fiancé, Adam, will be moving in," responded Caroline, watching the teenagers attentively.

"I didn't know that you're engaged," said Ruth.

"I've been engaged for more than two years," shared Caroline. "Maybe you'll get the chance to meet him soon!

He knows a lot of interesting stories," she bragged. "He's a college history professor."

"It'd be great..." Ruth paused to sip her juice. "Although we aren't really in the mood to learn about Gaia's history..."

"I understand... but you can't be depressed like that," advised Caroline, worried. "Albert, do you have any more clues about the dream?"

"No, nothing else," Albert mumbled. "It's clear that my parents are in total darkness, and confused about their fate. We're getting desperate too... but we still have no idea how to help..."

"When the time is right, you'll know what to do," Caroline comforted them.

"Dream? What are you talking about?" asked Nicolaus, mustard dripping down his chin.

"We kinda got warned about this situation by a dream. It's a long story..." said Albert. "Caroline, I'm a little embarrassed to ask, but do you like dogs?"

"I love dogs, Albert," Caroline responded. "Are you asking me if your dog can stay here?"

"I just don't want to leave Soap alone in our house..." he said.

"You can pick him up later if..." Caroline's eyes darted to a form hovering in the doorway. Violet, wearing a pink and white dress, was looking at them with a shy smile on her face.

"Sorry to surprise you like this, I just couldn't wait to see them," said Violet.

For a moment, Albert forgot all his sadness and smiled. Violet's presence always had that weird effect. Somehow she managed to bring out the best in him.

"Violet, you're also very welcome here! Please join us!" said Caroline, gesturing to Violet to come closer.

Violet walked towards the table and, one by one, hugged them all. Her hug was soft, cozy, and warm, vanishing Albert's pain.

Albert, Ruth, Nicolaus and Violet took the Zoom right after breakfast. Albert was glad to have Violet by his side as he entered his house. It simply didn't feel like home this time. He missed his parents' presence, their voices, and the emptiness of the place cut him deeply.

"Easy boy, we won't leave you here alone again." Albert petted an agitated Soap, who kept jumping on his legs.

"There's even more people than yesterday..." commented Ruth, after adjusting the wall to transparent-inside mode.

Almost a hundred protestors were gathered on their lawn. Some were sleeping, some still crying, and some just staring at their house, like they could see through the bricks and reach the eyes inside. Albert didn't blame them. They didn't know what had really happened. They just knew what they had been informed of by the news and the investigators. They were hurt. Pain like that could make anyone lose their senses and fall prey to base emotions.

"I've never seen this kind of thing in Gaia!" exclaimed Violet, scared.

"Neither have I..." said Nicolaus. "I can't believe Albert was warned about this craziness in a dream..."

"Albert, were you warned about your family's situation in a dream?" Violet asked, turning to look at Albert. "Why didn't you tell me anything?"

"I just found out too," Nicolaus chimed in.

"We were hoping that the dream was just a dream... not a Revelation." Albert stepped towards Violet.

"And after we confirmed the Revelation, we weren't in the mood to share..." Ruth confessed. "We just didn't know how to handle it."

"I understand," said Violet, turning back to face the crowd.

"I'm glad you understand," Albert whispered into Violet's ear. "The last thing I want is to hurt your feelings..."

The girl blushed and tried to recover her thoughts. "I'm glad you've been warned by a dream..." said Violet. "Revelations aren't just warnings though, they also show you that destiny can be changed."

"This is so confusing," said Albert. "I have no idea

how to help my parents. It's like my world is falling apart and my arms are tied."

"Just keep in mind that the key to a dream is your intuition," Violet emphasized. "If it says that your parents aren't guilty, then they really aren't."

"We should learn to follow our instincts like Soap..." Ruth thought out loud, pointing to a messy pile of chocolate-dog-food in the floor. The group laughed. "How did he find that package? The door is locked and his food server is outside, on the porch..."

"Guess he's smarter than we thought..." said Albert, holding the dog in his arm and walking back towards the garage.

As they arrived back at Caroline's house, Soap broke free, running around and making sure every item in the house was thoroughly inspected by his nose. When he saw Caroline in the living room, he jumped on the sofa to greet his new friend.

"Hello Soap," said Caroline quietly, with distant eyes. "Nice to meet you!" she patted the dog while he sniffed her hand.

"Is something wrong, Caroline?" asked Ruth, sitting on the sofa's edge.

Caroline swallowed and looked at Ruth. "Milet just called for a last minute session, and we're invited to attend."

"I hope it's not to declare the end of the investigation," said Albert, his inner turmoil returning.

"That would be bad for your parents," Caroline mumbled, facing the floor.

"Everything will be alright…" offered Violet, in an unsuccessful attempt to cheer them up. "I should go now… please call me after the meeting." She turned to Ruth.

"I will," promised Ruth, hugging her friend. "Thanks for your support."

"Yeah, that really means a lot to us," added Albert, trying to find in Violet's blue eyes the strength he needed.

TWELVE

The Council resembled a court room. High white chairs formed a circle, and in the center a huge circular floating light filled the interior with a yellowish-orange hue. When the trio arrived at the Council with Caroline, its members, including Julius and Randy, were already seated, dressed in formal white robes. The four suspects were seated in the center. Caroline and the teens took their seats in the guest area, close to the entrance. The meeting had just begun.

"Dear members of this Council," began Milet in a strong, calm voice. He stood in front of his chair. "The reason for this last minute meeting is the investigation of the burglary that resulted in the death of our former president – Ulysses. A couple of hours ago, Lionel brought me some serious accusations, which he must now share with all the members, as our regulations stipulate. We must listen to him calmly."

Lionel rose abruptly from his chair and stared hard at his audience. "Good evening, members of this Council. For personal reasons, I've been investigating my father's death with Randy's permission. I need to bring some important

153

facts to your attention. First of all, I'd like to ask Sophia to rise and tell us what she found at my father's house."

Sophia rose, straightened her hair, and turned to glance at Nicolaus before saying her statement. "There was another person in Ulysses's residence on the night of the crime," said Sophia. "Victor and George were framed by the real criminal!" she shouted.

"I returned to my father's house immediately after their arrest, a few minutes before six o'clock in the morning, with the most effective flashlight laser that I could find, and I can testify to the truth of what she said," reported Lionel. "The first part only, as they *weren't* framed," he emphasized.

"What do you mean with the first part only?" blurted Sophia indignantly, rising from her chair. "They *were* framed! They were!"

The council members glanced at each other.

"Sophia, I ask you to kindly respect this Council session by remaining silent, except when a question is addressed to you," Milet said firmly. "I understand that you're very emotional, but those are the rules."

Frowning, Sophia obeyed.

"I'd like to ask Dr. Framon to rise," Lionel proceeded. "As you all know, he is the head of the medical team responsible for the laboratory analysis of the suspects' blood. Could you please tell us the results?"

Dr. Framon, a slim man with broad shoulder and bad

posture, rose from his chair. He slightly straightened his white blazer before reading his notes. "We found in the blood samples a prohibited Intensifier."

"Could you please tell us what kind of Intensifier and what it does?" asked Lionel, walking towards the suspects in the center of the circle.

"The substance increases anger and frustration up to one's very breaking point," said Dr. Framon, looking at the suspects.

"But is this substance capable of making someone act against their will?" inquired Lionel.

"What kind of question is that?" shouted Sophia. "Of course it does! My husband would never commit a crime of his own free will!"

"Sophia, please behave yourself, or you won't be allowed to participate in these proceedings any longer," Milet scolded. "Dr. Framon, please respond to Lionel's question. Can this Intensifier distort a person's thoughts and encourage him to do something he otherwise wouldn't?"

"No, absolutely not," responded the doctor. "This intensifier only brings out what's inside of you. It can't make you break your principles or do something you'd never be capable of otherwise. However, if you were already planning something but felt too afraid to do it, this would eliminate those barriers."

"Thank you, Doctor," offered Lionel. "Ladies and gentlemen, based on this medical report, I ask for your authorization to bring a new suspect to this case – Julius Alsky."

Albert almost fell out of his chair. Ruth immediately reached for his hand, but this time he could offer no emotional support. Did he really hear it right? Julius, a criminal? Would that be even possible?

"He's been their sponsor and accompanied these families since the beginning," continued Lionel, who had been standing in front of Julius. "He knows their weaknesses and daily routines."

Julius faced Lionel's stare. "The fact that I know a lot about these families can't make me the main suspect!"

"Sure it can!" Lionel raised his tone of voice. "When you felt it was the right moment to act, you provoked Victor's frustrations. A few hours before the crime, Julius had class at the Kleins' house. He had the opportunity to put an illegal substance in Victor's drink, intensifying his anger. Coincidence or not, I've also heard that on that same day, Julius had lunch with George. Am I right, George?"

George, uncomfortable with the situation, leaned slightly forward in his chair. "That's correct, Lionel."

"Did the lunch take place before or after your argument with your supervisor?" asked Lionel, walking towards George.

"That question is unfounded!" Julius objected to Milet. But the new president signaled for George to answer.

"It was before," informed George. "We had lunch together, and a few hours after that, I had an argument with my boss."

"So that explains everything!" Lionel exclaimed. "Victor and George broke into my father's house to steal the documents. While one searched the first floor, the other went up to check the bedroom. My father woke up to the sound of someone rummaging through his things and had a heart attack. George and Victor finished their job, collecting all the secret data. What they didn't know is that the documents were protected by a powerful chemical compound. But Julius did. He waited for the chemical to knock them out to steal the documents from them."

"That makes sense," interjected Randy. "Except that the data wasn't missing," he continued in a condescending tone. "All documents were found next to the suspects."

"I didn't rob Ulysses!" Julius protested.

"Randy, it's quite simple," continued Lionel. "With special gloves, Julius copied all the secret data to his MOD and left George and Victor unconscious in the street, with all of the evidence of their crime beside them."

"These are very serious accusations, Lionel." Milet leaned back on his chair. He looked at Julius, then back at Lionel, reflecting. "I guess we could verify this allegation now. Julius, please give your MOD to Randy."

"Are you serious, Sir?" asked Julius, bitterly. Milet nodded.

Dragging his feet, Julius rose from chair, walked towards Randy and handed over his device. He stared angrily at Lionel before returning to his seat.

With fast fingers and under everyone's curious gaze, Randy began examining the device, pausing a few seconds to read its contents. He glanced up at Milet, unsure if he could even pronounce his next statement.

"Randy, your thoughts would be very much appreciated," asked Milet.

"The allegations are true," said Randy, turning to Julius.

"It isn't possible! I never saw these documents!" claimed Julius. "Why don't you analyze my memory and verify what I'm saying?"

"You don't think we'll fall into that trap, do you?" snapped Lionel. "Anyone with your knowledge can control emotions and memories."

"Lionel is right, Julius," Milet agreed. "What guarantee do we have that you won't block access to certain memories and create others? You're an expert in self-control."

"But I have to say that this is a little absurd…" intervened Randy. "Why would Julius want access to secret information?"

Albert suspected that Randy's comment had less to do with determining Julius's motives and more with his frustration over not having figured it out himself.

"To answer this question, I'll reveal a fact that I've been investigating for some time..." said Lionel.

"Lionel, I'm afraid you didn't tell me anything about a parallel investigation..." Milet interrupted.

"More secret investigation, Lionel?" questioned Randy. "I'm the Chief Investigator, I should be advised of all investigations that are taking place!"

"My mistake Milet and Randy, but please, allow me to share what I've uncovered," Lionel apologized. "I assure you it will be quite enlightening."

As Milet gestured in agreement, Lionel continued. "Julius has been going to Earth without permission, disrespecting our rule that all travel to Earth should be approved by the president and all members of this Council. Something as planned and hidden as this can only prove Julius's intention: He wanted to take all the secret information to Earth, where he would reveal it in order to be considered a genius and idolized as a king. Ambition was his motive."

Scattered voices echoed around the room. The members looked shocked and confused.

"Julius, is that true?" asked Milet. "Have you been visiting Earth without our consent? Yes or no?"

"Yes, Milet, for the past two years," confessed Julius. The buzz increased. "But let me explain," he asked, rising from his chair. "As you know, I came to Gaia very young, when Ulysses took me from my orphanage on Earth. All that time I was raised by Ulysses's cousin Marta, who died a few years back. I've always believed that my real family was dead. But exactly two years ago, my life and everything that I used to believe was turned upside down."

"Why are you telling us this?" asked Milet. "How is this relevant to this case?"

"Ulysses confessed that he was my father," said Julius.

The commotion among those present became uncontrollable.

"You lie!" shouted Lionel.

"I was the result of a relationship he had on Earth with a poor young Earth woman. She couldn't raise me and gave me up for adoption," said Julius. "Ulysses said he couldn't live far away from me, so he brought me to Gaia, but he never had the courage to tell about his relationship with my mother to anyone; he didn't want to cause suffering to his wife and son with his lies and betrayal."

"You're making this up!" accused a furious Lionel.

"My visits to Earth occurred after I learned the truth," continued Julius. "I went to Earth with Ulysses's approval; he covered my trip so that no one would suspect anything. I've been visiting my mother regularly since then."

The members kept talking among themselves, and Milet was forced to rise from his chair to be heard. "I must end the accusations for today. We have much to investigate and many facts to be checked. Due to the new evidence, though, Julius will have to be placed under arrest. Victor and George will remain in the IC, as you're still guilty, given that the Intensifier only made you do what you had already planned." He took a deep breath before continuing. "Sarah and Sophia are still suspects as well."

"I'd just like to add that I could never plan a crime and place the blame on someone else," said Julius. "I always liked the Beckers and Kleins, they were my friends!"

"You didn't even defend them! What kind of friend are you?" attacked Lionel.

"Julius and Lionel, I said this is enough for one day!" Milet interjected. "I want to make it clear that I'll do everything in my power to see the truth revealed as soon as possible. Good night, everyone."

Albert really wanted to run up to Julius and demand a decent explanation from him, but he was immediately escorted out of the room by guards, along with his parents. Acting on a whim, he walked towards Lionel instead, and pointed straight at his face. "Look, I'll prove to you that my dad and my mom are innocent. Just wait and see."

Lionel stared at Albert, then pushed his finger down. "Show me some proof and I'll be on your side. The only thing I really want is to find the truth. I owe this to my father," he said, pacing out of the room and leaving Albert speechless.

Reflecting upon everything that was said at the meeting, the teenagers followed Caroline to her house. The teacher set the dinner table in complete silence, respecting their sorrow. The silence remained throughout the dinner.

It was hard not to feel disappointed. To think that Julius had been lying to them since the beginning was sharply painful to Albert. He felt stabbed in the back... trapped... but at the same time he blamed himself. How could he be so naïve and such a bad judge of people's character? How could he have trusted Julius so easily? How? It didn't matter now... their parents were already taken in and exploited. But were they taken in completely? Something inside him refused to believe that his dad was a criminal, but he couldn't ignore the doctor's words. The Intensifier could only make someone do what they were already planning. His dad was a scientist... someone who would always be driven to find new answers and ways to help society thrive through technology. But would his curiosity be deep enough to supersede his other values? Would he jeopardize his family just to feed the hunger of his scientific mind?

"You know... It makes a lot of sense," Nicolaus broke the silence. "It's like pieces of a puzzle... Julius was motivated by his ambition, his bitterness and his jealousy."

"Yeah, that makes sense..." agreed Ruth, playing with the rest of the food on her plate. "But how could we prove that Julius acted by himself, and that our parents are innocent?"

"Is there any chance of that medical report be wrong, Caroline?" asked Albert. "Could the doctor be mistaken?"

"I don't believe so," said Caroline, trying to find the rights words. "An entire group of prestigious doctors were behind this medical report. Although Dr. Framon was the one in charge, he didn't come to that conclusion by himself."

"You know... I'm so confused with all this..." confessed Albert. "Why did I have that dream if I can't find a solution? Maybe the dream was just to prepare myself psychologically for failure... It seems like there's nothing we can do to help!"

"Maybe you can help Lionel with his investigations," suggested Caroline.

"Do you think so?" questioned Albert, sipping his juice.

Caroline leaned over on the table. "Do you want me to say what I'm really thinking?"

"Yes, please, Caroline," asked Ruth.

"Lionel seems to have a point, but... I've known Julius for a long time... he helped me and my father with our transfer to Gaia... His eyes are full of kindness and caring..."

"I know what you mean..." said Nicolaus, the only one having dessert – a strawberry pudding topped with mint ice-cream.

"I know you have a deep belief in your parents' innocence, but how do you feel about Julius?" asked Caroline.

The kids stayed quiet for a moment, reflecting.

"I think you should follow your intuition. That's my only suggestion…" continued Caroline. She sipped her water and her face lit up. "Albert, don't you remember any other detail from your dream? Did you tell us everything, exactly as it happened?"

"Yeah, I told you everything..." said Albert. The question upset him. The truth was that he was tired of all this *dream talk*. He didn't want a *gift* that had no use other than making him feel nervous in advance and frustrated for not being able to decipher it correctly when there were other people's lives at stake, depending on him. "I didn't leave any relevant details out," Albert promised, while feeding his leftover dinner to Soap.

"Did you consider any detail irrelevant?" asked Caroline, intrigued.

He tried to disguise his impatience. "There was a sort of background sound in my dream… But it didn't make any sense..."

"What was it?" asked Caroline.

"Something I never heard before, I didn't think it was a word because I couldn't find it in any dictionary…" He tried to dig deep into his unconscious. "The sound that kept repeating was something like, *raif*..." he told them, in an effort to put an end on the subject.

"Raif?" repeated Caroline, looking pale. "Why didn't I think about that before?"

"What are you talking about?" inquired Nicolaus, his spoon frozen midair.

"I need to confirm a few facts before I say anything more. I don't want to jump to conclusions. It's very late, but I'll arrange a meeting tomorrow with my fiancé," said Caroline, rising from her chair and leaving the room with distant eyes. The teenagers remained at the table, looking at each other, concerned and confused.

THIRTEEN

"**H**ow did you convince Caroline to let us miss class to-day?" asked a surprised Nicolaus to Violet.

Sitting on the sofa with Ruth and Nicolaus, Albert analyzed Violet's movements and expressions attentively. There was something off with her... he noticed that since she'd arrived at Caroline's house that morning, talking without pause and avoiding eye contact. She looked frail, restless, and sad... just like him.

"I just told Caroline that I had a really good reason and that she should trust me..." Violet responded. "She just made me promise that you would be back here right after sunset. She said something about her fiancé..."

"So what's so important that you had to talk to us?" asked Albert.

"I have a plan..." began Violet, looking at Ruth. "I've always learned that there is no perfect crime; I bet that the criminal did something wrong and we need to find out what it is..."

"Violet, we can't invade Ulysses's house again," Ruth

166

cut her off. "Randy is probably still monitoring the house."

"I know about the people detector," continued Violet, nervously passing her long fingers through her hair. "Yesterday I kept thinking about how Soap found the package of chocolate dog food you guys hid, and then I remembered him sniffing around Caroline's house when we got here..."

"Wait a minute, are you saying that Soap should break into Ulysses's house to investigate?" asked Nicolaus, laughing. A sharp look from Violet forced him to take her seriously.

"Ulysses's dog died just a few years ago, so there's a special entrance for dogs, out back. Soap could use this entrance to search for clues by himself!" suggested Violet.

"But, Violet, how will Soap search the house? He's a dog. He just sniffs around!" said Albert, cautiously.

"Great, that's what we need!" Violet crouched to pet Soap. "I know it sounds crazy, but we don't have options. My idea is simple! I'll explain everything on our way to the Botanical Garden."

"Botanical Garden?" repeated Ruth, confused.

"Yeah, that's right!" she said, without further explanation.

The entrance was breathtaking. Calla Lilies surrounded a peaceful green lake, filled by two small waterfalls. A glass bridge led them between the falls to the flower gardens.

Albert felt a strong urge to lie down, close his eyes, and let the sun shine away all his problems while he focused on the sound of the falls. His whole body seemed to calm as he took in his surroundings, far away from the trouble's that had brought them here.

The colorful oasis was divided by two pathways surrounded by tall trees. As they chose one to follow, their presence caught the attention of a few employees, carefully pruning the flowers.

"Maybe we should split..." suggested Ruth, diverting her eyes from a worker's gaze.

"I agree," said Violet. "We can't make them think that we're up to something... I'll walk with Albert and Soap on the other path... both will lead us to the same place. That way they'll think we're just boyfriends and girlfriends enjoying a romantic tour..." she held Albert's hand and pulled him towards the other sidewalk.

As they walked down the path, passing tulips of all colors and sizes, Albert's heart started racing up again. How he wished they were there under different circumstances... her cold hands touching his and that breathtaking place made him feel disoriented. The girl by his side meant so much to him that the idea of losing her numbed his whole body. Chances were that he would be leaving Gaia soon... without even having the chance to tell her how he really felt.

"You didn't have to do this for us, Violet," said Albert.

He bent down, picked up a red tulip and put it behind Violet's ear. "You shouldn't be taking risks..."

"Yes, I should..." Violet cut him off. "Do you think I would be okay if I wound up losing my best friends forever? If you guys go back to Earth, you won't remember Gaia, you won't remember me... but I'll have to learn how to live with the pain of losing you... I'd be broken inside for year and years..."

"I don't want to forget your face, Violet..." Albert stopped and stared at Violet's eyes. "I don't want to forget you... and I don't think anything or anyone could ever make me."

Violet sprang into Albert's arms. He hugged her tightly, trying to protect her from all that pain. When she let him go, he wiped her tears with his finger and softly kissed her cheek. He focused on her to gauge her response, but her face was inscrutable.

"We should go now..." said Violet, recomposing herself. "We don't want to make them wait..." She held his hand and resumed her steps.

She was completely silent for the rest of their walk. He didn't mind, though. It wasn't necessary – they both had said enough already.

After a few more flower beds and sculptured trees, they arrived at a hedge with gray roses, which seemed to signalize the end of the path.

"Where are they?" asked Albert, looking around.

"Pssst, here!" a muffled voice drew their attention.

"Did you already jump the hedge?" Violet whispered, making sure they weren't being watched.

"You took too long!" replied Nicolaus, his face appearing from behind the hedge. "We couldn't stay there and wait..."

Albert grabbed Soap in his arm and quickly handed the dog to Nicolaus, who then returned to hiding. After helping Violet, Albert gave a few steps back to boost his impulse. But when he finally jumped the hedge, his right leg got trapped by the thorns.

"That's okay, man, I'll help you!" whispered Nicolaus, pulling Albert's arms with all his strength.

As Albert felt the thorns rip his skin, he let out a muffled scream.

"Thanks a lot for that, Nicolaus..." Albert ragged.

"No need for thanks, you know I always got your back!" said Nicolaus, extending his fist for a friendly bump.

Albert left him hanging and scanned their surroundings. He had to admit that it was a clever way to get to the back of Ulysses's house. They were now safe from the gardeners' view, and the numerous trees in the backyard offered the privacy they needed to carry out their plan.

"The entrance for Soap is right there," Violet remarked, pointing to a dog-sized entry in the wall. After removing the flowers that covered it, she confirmed it wasn't locked.

"Wow, I'd never have noticed this door if you hadn't pointed it out!" said Ruth, emerging from behind a tree and crawling towards the house.

Focusing hard, Violet held Soap in her lap and put a small device the size of a button on his nose. Soap licked it for a while and then stopped.

"Now it's time for the Smell Intensifier..." said Violet, grabbing an I-shaped bottle from her pocket along with a cookie. After pouring the whole contents of the bottle on the cookie, she let Soap eat half of it. The other half she threw inside the house, through the dog door. Soap fell into her trap and flew inside to hunt the food.

Violet then enlarged her MOD, and the others sat close by to watch the images that were already being transmitted back by Soap.

Soap began his investigation in the living-room, smelling intensively a sofa, a houseplant, a light-green rug and also a coffee table.

Although the transmission was of a high quality, the dim light of the room and the way Soap quickly walked and moved his head, were making a little hard to see everything.

"So that's how a dog sees the world!" Nicolaus laughed.

Soap proceeded towards the dining-room, where he made sure to smell every single leg of all chairs that encircled the table. Afterwards, he decided to check the corners of the cupboard, where he found some scraps of food. The prospect of anything else to eat led him to carefully recheck the whole room.

"Could this be any more boring?" complained Nicolaus. "Violet, you don't happen to have another cookie with you, do you?"

She gave him a disapproving look.

"What? I channel all my stress into eating. Food and I have a very complex relationship."

Soap went up the wood stairs. In Ulysses's bedroom Soap decided to sniff some clothes on top of an armchair. The dog's reaction drew their attention.

"Why is he sniffing those clothes like that?" Violet inquired.

"He always sniffs our clothes, today won't be any different..." said Albert.

"And now he is back to sniffing the floor..." Violet narrated Soap's movements, with her eyes fixed on the screen.

"What is that?" Ruth interjected, pointing to a blurry shape.

The four friends pressed together to get a better look.

"Just a flip flop under the bed, no big deal..." said Albert.

"So maybe the criminal didn't leave any traces..." said

Violet, frustrated with the clean floor.

"Wait!" Nicolaus exclaimed. "What is Soap doing?"

"Oh my..." Violet interjected. "Don't tell me that... he just jumped onto the bed!"

The blue sheets of Ulysses's bed were taking the entire screen.

"Soap, do you really want to sleep right now?" grumbled Ruth, ashamed.

"He's just a dog who loves being in bed..." said Albert. It was hard to keep a straight face. He was feeling like a fool, watching a dog wander in a house in the hope that he wouldn't act like an animal, but as some sort of Special Forces agent in a top secret mission... this was stupid... "We can't expect too much from him..." he continued, hoping the rest would agree to call off the attempt. But nobody responded. They didn't even blink. The scratches caused by thorns seemed to burn under the sun, and he started to feel out of sorts.

"Look!" said Violet, pointing to an object probed by his nose. "Am I crazy or...?"

"Is it a necklace? Can you get a close up of the image, Violet?" asked Ruth.

Violet zoomed in, and a small broken gold chain and pendant filled the screen. They could now see the pendant's engraved image — a dragon spitting fire.

"Albert, this figure is identical to that drawing Isadora

sent us," recalled Ruth.

Albert nodded. He couldn't believe that the dog had just proved him wrong.

"As far as I know, that's a very old symbol..." said Violet. "My mother keeps track of illegal documents for the Council. One day... when I barged into her office and she was examining some files, I remember seeing that exact same image..."

"So it's illegal?" asked Nicolaus.

"Yes, it is," Violet confirmed. "When I asked her about it, she said that the documents were confidential and that she couldn't go into details, but she said it was an image banned across Gaia, a symbol of prejudice and hate."

"The chain probably belonged to Ulysses's secret archives, and the criminal left it there," Albert concluded.

"It couldn't belong to Ulysses's archives," said Violet. "Banned and confiscated documents don't stay with the President, and Ulysses would never own this kind of thing. He always did everything he could to put an end to discrimination..."

"I guess we've reached a conclusion: The necklace must belong to the criminal," said Nicolaus. "But how are we going to grab it? We can't enter the house to pick it up!" he raised his voice and was shushed by his friends.

"We don't need to get the necklace..." whispered Violet. "We just need to investigate who the owner could be.

"And it seems like we already have a lead, right?" Nicolaus added.

"I wonder how come Isadora knows the meaning of the image... that's really weird," said Violet.

"I think I know where we should go next to investigate..." said Ruth, shaking a few leaves off her clothes.

"First we need to give Soap a reason to leave," said Violet, putting some chocolate dog food at the entrance. Through her MOD, they could see Soap sniffing intently and exiting the bedroom. "I'm sorry I can't go with you, though... My mom thinks that I'm at school, so I need to be home on time."

"You've already helped us a lot, Violet," Ruth hugged her friend. "Now it's my time to use my gift..."

"What are you talking about?" questioned Albert.

"Well, your gift alerted you to this whole thing, Albert. And I hope my gift can be useful now..." she said, without further explanations.

FOURTEEN

The sun was low in the sky. The cold winds reddened their faces, making their wait all the more uncomfortable. For more than an hour they were on full alert, searching for their target. Maybe it hadn't been that long, pondered Albert. His anxiety had probably altered his perception of time. He felt like a criminal, hidden behind yet another tree on his school's lawn, but he knew that things could easily spin out of control if anyone discovered them. Watching those familiar faces happily leaving the school grounds made Albert feel even more miserable and, for a moment, he envied them. Not their lives, but their naivety and the absolute trust they had in other people. He figured sadly that regardless of the outcome of recent events, he wouldn't dare to open himself like that again.

"Our target is alone," reported Nicolaus, lying on the floor and using his MOD as a pair of binoculars. He seemed to be enjoying his task. "That sure makes things easier for us."

"Please stay here you two," ordered Ruth. "I prefer to do it by myself."

"Are you sure?" Albert whispered to Ruth. Although he trusted her insightful plan, he felt the need to protect his sister now more than ever.

"Yeah… Ulysses said that people are honest with me… so I'll just have to rely on that…" said Ruth.

"Get going!" said Nicolaus, gesturing wildly.

Ruth stepped out from behind the tree and made herself visible, walking alongside Phin.

After a few steps, Phin stopped, surprised. "Hey! It's good to see you… I was worried..." he said, analyzed Ruth's face. "How are you doing?"

"I'm fine, just trying to survive…" replied Ruth, staring at the floor.

"Is there anything I can do?" he asked sympathetically, putting his hand on her forearm.

"Actually, yes," she said Ruth, gathering courage. "I need some information… I was hoping that you…"

"What is it? Shoot!"

Ruth took a deep breath, deciding to go straight to the point. "When my dad got arrested, Isadora sent me a picture of a dragon spitting fire and..."

"And since I used to date Isadora, you think..." Phin cut her off.

"Well, I can't count on Isadora's help..." She stared at his gray eyes. "Did she show it to you before?"

"No… she didn't…" said Phin, diverting his eyes from Ruth's gaze, but not in time to avoid revealing his reluctance.

"But have you seen this dragon picture before?" she insisted.

"No… not with her…"

She grasped his hand. "Phin, I'm not going to get you in trouble, I promise… But please, this information is very important... Do you know anything about it? Anything?"

"More or less... I mean, I've seen the dragon, but not with Isadora," Phin hesitated.

"Where have you seen it?" inquired Ruth, reading his eyes.

Phin sighed, then looked around to make sure they weren't being watched. "One night, when I was eating dinner at Isadora's house, her dad leaned forward to sit down and a chain he was wearing fell out of his shirt… he grabbed it right away… but I saw the picture on it first…"

Ruth quickly handed her MOD to Phin. "Can you tell me if this was the necklace that Lionel used?" she asked, showing him the saved image.

Phin held the device and analyzed the picture for a few seconds. "It's identical…" he paused, as if unsure if he should share more. Ruth met his glance, trying to melt his doubts away, and to assure him that there was no reason why he should keep anything from her. "I… asked Isadora... a few days later... about the meaning of the necklace..." he continued. "She told me it was the symbol of Gaia's perfect population."

"Perfect population? She didn't tell you anything more?" Ruth insisted.

"No, she just said that," assured Phin.

"How strange..." She took her device back, shrunk it, and put it on her jeans' pocket. "Well, thank you so much, you helped me a lot... I have to go now..." said Ruth. As she turned to leave, Phin stopped her, taking her hand.

"I've been thinking about you a lot, since our last meeting..." said Phin, pulling Ruth towards him. "I'd love to have dinner with you again..."

"I'm sorry, but... my life is upside down right now..." said Ruth, trying to disguise the pain in her voice.

"I know and I'm sorry about everything..." He slightly caressed her hand. "I hope it all works out."

Ruth let a few seconds pass, allowing herself be lost in his eyes. She then put her hand on his chest and kindly kissed him on the cheek. "Thanks," she whispered, releasing her hand from his grasp and walking away.

After looking over her shoulder to confirm that Phin was walking, Ruth returned to the tree where Albert, Nicolaus and Soap remained hidden. But they didn't seem to notice her presence.

"Is something wrong?" she asked, noticing that their

eyes were glued to their MODs' screens.

"We were reading the news..." said Albert, flatly. "Seems that Julius just tried to escape..."

"What?" Ruth crouched to glance at their devices.

"He claims this isn't true... but it's hard to deny facts, right?" said Nicolaus, petting Soap.

"The news is saying that the authorities are now even more convinced of his guilt..." commented Albert.

Ruth leaned against the tree. "I don't know what to think... Now I'm even more confused..."

"Why? What did Phin say?" inquired Albert, curious.

"I'll tell you everything over at Caroline's house... it's already time for the meeting she set up with her fiancé..."

Caroline had prepared an interesting surprise. As they stepped into the living room, a slight breeze welcomed them through the dimming light. As they felt their feet sink into the bright sand, which replaced the hard floor, they immediately noticed the smell of sea air and the sound of waves mixed with the chirping of crickets. Soap instantly started howling and running around circles. He then stopped to dig the sand.

The living room sofa gave way to five beach chairs that were encircling a floating silver platter giving off flames.

"Bonfire!" exclaimed Ruth, admiring Caroline's arrangements.

"Yeah, I figured you might be feeling a little homesick today, so... I hope you enjoy!" said Caroline, rising from her chair.

"That's awesome!" Nicolaus rushed to sit close to the fire.

"Nicolaus, where's your manners, man?" Albert reprehended his friend. "It's really nice to meet you..." he said extending his hand to Caroline's fiancé, who was standing right next to her, with a friendly smile.

"Nice to meet you too, I'm Adam," he said, with a strong hand shake. His brown shoulder-length hair falling over his eyes.

"So you're Caroline's fiancé!" said Ruth. "She was bragging the other day about you..."

"Is that so?" asked Adam, with a crooked smile.

"Of course, I'm really proud of you!" Caroline kissed Adam on his cheek. "I'm glad you're all here, I was getting worried!"

"Well, it was a long day..." Ruth sighed, rubbing her hands together close to the flames. "We'll tell you everything... but first, let's enjoy our bonfire!"

The warmth provided by the flames was exactly what Albert needed that night. It actually made him relax and breathe, putting aside for a while the pressure that had burdened him. The moon above the transparent ceiling reminded him of life's cycles and how everything was transient.

Events could take sudden turns, certain facts could have new interpretations, and people's true colors could be revealed. Life would always be unpredictable, and time would prove it. He knew it was only a matter of patience and perseverance.

Enjoying marshmallows with chocolate and sipping a strong hot tea, they got to know more about Caroline's fiancé.

Adam was one of those people whose passion for life seemed to overflow. He easily captivated the attention of a room, with his graphic, gripping stories and words emphasized like they were picked specially for the occasion.

Defining himself as a man who loved to find the truth behind facts, Adam confessed that he inherited his passion from his father, who would discuss with him for hours about Gaia and Earth's history, motivating his studies of mysterious stories and controversies.

Adam's charisma and eloquence fascinated the young group and a bond formed quickly between them. With attentive eyes, he listened to Albert and Ruth narrate what they had found that day. When they finished, Adam leaned forward in his chair; his eyes shining. It took him a few minutes to finally respond.

"I'm very impressed with your investigative work, guys..." said Adam, looking deeply into each of their eyes. "It's quite unbelievable..."

"You took too many risks!" complained Caroline. "But

you were very creative and smart... I couldn't be more proud."

"It doesn't seem to matter now, after the latest news about Julius... Maybe we were following the wrong trail, that's all..." Ruth vented.

"Yeah, we heard the news about Julius... Things are pretty ugly for him..." Caroline confirmed.

"But what happened? How did he try to escape?" Ruth asked.

"Seems that he pretended to be dizzy, falling on the floor while he talked to the Chief Investigator," said Caroline. "Randy thought he had fainted, so he bent down to help him, but Julius knocked him unconscious."

"Wow! I didn't know Julius had ninja skills!" Nicolaus laughed at his own joke, while putting some melted chocolate on a big loaf of bread and toasting it on the fire before eating it.

Caroline ignored the comment. "Julius grabbed Randy's MOD and put it on the wall, so he could exit the room. But Randy recovered his senses just in time to prevent the escape."

"Now he's in big trouble..." Adam concluded. "Randy made a statement that he was trying to prove Julius's innocence, but now he's learned that Julius wasn't the good guy he'd always trusted. Randy said that Julius's eyes were wide open when he attacked him, full of rage, and his teeth were clenched. He said he would try to proceed with an impartial investigation, despite his disappointment."

"The investigators are now saying that this kind of behavior leads them to believe that Julius has a mental disorder," added Sarah. "The News is exploring this theory to the fullest."

"This is too weird for me now…" Albert thought out loud.

"And do you want to know what is even weirder, Albert?" Caroline paused, creating more suspense. "I invited Adam over to explain the meaning of the word you heard in your dream… 'Raif'."

"The meaning is right in front of you," Adam offered, leaving Albert puzzled.

"I'm not very good with riddles or metaphors," confessed Albert, a bit impatiently.

"It's literally in front of you," said Adam, with a smile.

Albert reflected for a moment, while grabbing another marshmallow and sticking it on the tip of a long metal fork. As he watched it gradually turn brown, it hit him.

"Raif is *fire* backwards… I mean, it's the sound of the word backwards," Albert deciphered.

Adam nodded. "And not only that. Raif is also the name of an old symbol – The opulent Dragon."

Ruth and Albert stopped eating and looked at each other. Nicolaus choked, and had to spit out a piece of bread into the fire.

Adam continued. "The meaning behind it is simple: it represents racial purification through fire."

"'Purification through fire'?" repeated Ruth, waiting for more explanation.

"The fire destroys, kills; it symbolizes annihilation," said Adam, throwing a piece of bread on the flames and watching it vanish. "Fire is also the only one of the four elements that can be produced by man. The Dragon represents the defender of the Gaian race, which should put an end to everything and everyone that are hazardous to the welfare of this pure society."

"This dragon dates back from the time of Atlantis, when mystics and dreamers were hated and seen as a corrupting and disgraceful influence by an extremist group – the creators of the Raif symbolism," added Caroline, holding Soap on her lap.

"During this time, mystics of Secret Science were their target," said Adam. "Things only changed when the dream that predicted the final disaster of Atlantis had its authenticity confirmed."

"So this group ended just before they came to Gaia?" asked Albert, almost holding his breath not to miss anything.

"No, the clan continued... but with another target: The Chosen," said Adam, making the young group suddenly lose their appetite. "When the immigration system started, years after the population moved to Gaia, some people opposed it. They thought that Gaia should follow its own path."

"But this group of people didn't attack the Chosen, right?" asked Nicolaus, trying to remember the rumors that he had heard before. Nothing had seemed that serious.

"No, they didn't," confirmed Caroline. "Except for an extremist minority... Don't you recall any of the scary stories in our literature textbook about missing Chosens, Nicolaus?"

Nicolaus eyes widened. "Are they true?"

Adam locked his mug between his hands and slowly sipped the drink, as if it could help him choose the right words. "The Raif clan reemerged to end immigration and the link between Earth and Gaia, they made the Chosen's life miserable during their first days in Gaia, doing everything in their power to make the candidates give up," said Adam. "And even committing crimes... We always hear the saying that for more than two centuries a serious crime doesn't happen in Gaia... Do you know what occurred 200 years ago? Almost half of the Chosen families disappeared without leaving a trace... the clan also acted to erase any information about Atlantis and Gaia that might still be on Earth."

"Some Egyptians descendants of Atlantis didn't want the story of the island to be forgotten after their deaths,"

Caroline explained, while caressing Soap's ears. "So they built secret chambers to hide records about Atlantis, written on papyrus in code. They believed that if a person was smart enough to find the chamber, he'd deserve to know about Atlantis."

"But the Raif members couldn't tolerate the idea of someone on Earth knowing the truth about Atlantis and Gaia," continued Adam. "They looted the three majestic pyramids of Giza, and many years later..." Adam shook his head, his eyes full of indignation. "They destroyed one of the wonders of the ancient world... the Library of Alexandria."

"Are you saying that they were the ones who burned it down?" inquired Albert, his mind picturing it all like a movie. He could see a small and well coordinated group with torches in their hands, angrily setting fire to the library at dawn, and laughing ominously while watching it turn to ashes.

Adam poured himself and Caroline more tea, adding a bit of honey to the drink, then sipped it calmly. His long pause was met with impatience by the young group.

"In order to have the biggest and most important library of that time, the coordinators had an audacious idea: Each ship that docked at Alexandria would be monitored," explained Adam, as if giving a lecture. "If they found any written work on a ship, the owner was required to provide a copy. In many cases, the original copy was confiscated.

That way, several secret documents that were under the possession of descendants of Atlantis ended up in the hands of the dock inspector in Alexandria, and, consequently, were sent to the Library."

"So it's not a coincidence that people on Earth don't know about Atlantis, only rumors…" Nicolaus sighed. "Do you think Ulysses was their victim too?"

Adam shook his head. "I don't think he was the target. The group didn't want to kill Ulysses, but to forge a robbery and frame the Chosen."

"But why, out of all the Chosen, just our families?" questioned Ruth.

"The decision wasn't personal," Adam opined. "The group had bigger plans, not just the arrest of your parents; they planned to incite the whole population to remove all immigrants once and for all."

"So, all the evidence leads us to believe that Lionel is a member of the clan, right?" concluded Albert.

"That's right," Adam agreed.

"Maybe Julius is also a Raif member," suggested Ruth. "We can't forget that the investigation in place indicates that Julius was in Ulysses's house on the night of the crime… how can we be sure that he didn't wear a chain like Lionel's?"

"But Julius is a Chosen…" replied Nicolaus, confused.

"Yes, he is, but maybe he regrets it…" said Ruth.

"Maybe he despises the fact that someone took him from Earth and away from his mother, dragging him into a new planet and into a life he didn't want. Maybe he really hates the immigration system and what it did to him and wants to destroy it."

The group reflected for a moment, while watching Soap asleep under Caroline's caressing hands. Ruth's hypotheses combined all the possible clues they had and did make a lot of sense. Julius could have used them from the beginning to achieve his goal. That could be the reason he volunteered to be their sponsor in their selection process and personally tutor his parents. He was just playing a cruel game with them and waiting for the right moment to act.

Ruth could have simply solved the mystery, Albert realized. But at the same time he still felt crushed. Although he knew that proving Julius's guilt wouldn't prove their dads' innocence, it should at least give him some sort of comfort for being on the right track. Instead he was even more anguished and torn.

"Are you okay, Albert?" asked Caroline, bringing him back from his trance.

"Yeah, I'm just trying to understand why..." Albert began. "Why someone could be so cold and heartless... how people can use others to achieve their goals no matter how many lies they have to spread and how many lives they could ruin." Albert couldn't disguise the anger in his voice. "No matter what happens, I just don't think I'm going to be the same person anymore... I'm not sure if I'll be able to be close to people like I used to want to be... this whole thing made me see that I can't completely trust... just letting people into my life and allowing them to fool me like that. They can crush us without hesitation or remorse..."

Caroline rose from her chair and hugged Albert. "Hey, please don't think that way... don't let anyone or anything change the goodness and sincerity inside of you..."

Soap followed Caroline and showed his affection by licking Albert's face.

"She's right," said Adam, putting down his mug and staring into Albert's eyes. "People can be very tricky. Some are hardened by life, growing up bitter and empty... it's weird, but some can find pleasure from others' pain... but others become the best parts of your life, they comfort you when you're hurt, and they bring you happiness without asking for anything in return. Just think about Caroline and how much she loves you guys, bringing you all here to her house and trying to protect you... think about Violet and how much she risked today just to help you. No matter where you are, you'll find all different types of people, the important thing is to not let them define who you are and always give them benefit of the doubt, letting them trust you and be trusted."

"You know... there's something that keeps bothering me..." interrupted Caroline. "Remember when Nicolaus bumped into Lionel at the IC, and his briefcase fell open?

Did any of you see what he had inside? It's so strange to see someone carrying a briefcase here..."

"I didn't see anything... I just helped Nicolaus..." Albert replied. "But I remember that Ruth handed him something, right?"

"Everything happened so fast..." said Ruth, digging back to that day. "Lionel didn't let me touch anything. I just managed to pick up his bottle of Intensifier – he practically grabbed it right out of my hand."

"Intensifier? What kind of Intensifier?" asked Caroline, with a serious expression.

"Just a red one... He said it was to give him patience," responded Ruth.

"Woah! I think we just found another clue..." Adam exclaimed, as he and Caroline turned to each other.

"Absolutely." Caroline smiled back.

"Intensifiers are always blue," Adam explained. "The samples that weren't approved after testing are left in red containers and can't be distributed. They're stored at the IC for safety."

"The thing is that just a few Intensifiers have been rejected recently," continued Caroline. "It just so happens one of them was found in your fathers' blood."

"So why would Lionel have that Intensifier in his possession?" Ruth questioned.

"That's a good question... and I'm sure he doesn't

have a good answer for it, otherwise he wouldn't have lied to you, saying it was for *patience*."

"What if we ask Randy to analyze Lionel's memories?" Nicolaus suggested.

"Lionel is perfectly capable of controlling his thoughts, just like Julius..." replied Adam. "The only way would be..."

Adam rose from his chair without finishing the sentence and crossed the room with quick steps.

"What?" asked Albert, almost yelling to be heard.

Adam yelled back over his shoulder. "Stay here, no matter what! I really hope this works."

FIFTEEN

Adam strode along the graveled path, feeling the adrenaline course through his veins. Only the crunching of his steps against the ground disturbed his focus. He had been there a few times before, when he wanted to be alone and miles away from civilization. Being in contact with nature was sometimes the only way he could relax and get perspective in challenging times. He tried to convince himself that being there at night wasn't much different from visiting in the daytime – but as the vegetation became denser and innumerable trees blocked his view, he was forced to change his mind. He had adjusted his outfit to cover his face from the sharp cold and set his shoes to glow, serving to illuminate a few steps, but it was hard not to get lost in the dark unknown. Soon the gravel was replaced with wet soil and the sound of nocturnal animals filled the air.

After a few more minutes of walking, Adam arrived at the spot – a clearing by the edge of a waterfall, surrounded by thick trees and high rocks. He chose a flat one and sat down, breathless and tired. The shriek of an owl sent him shivers. But he wasn't the type of person to surrender to his fears. Tonight he had a point to prove.

His guest was late, and it was starting to disturb him. He knew his plan was rushed, he hadn't devoted time to solidifying his strategy, but there wasn't much to think about. His strategy was simple, taken from his favorite card game. Bluff.

"Are you Adam?" a voice shot out from behind a tree.

"Yes, I am," he confirmed, trying to keep his cool – if his emotions took control, the consequences would be disastrous. Facing Lionel's stare, he readjusted his clothes to reveal his face.

"I received your message to meet here," said Lionel, keeping a safe distance. "What do you want to tell me about my father's death?"

"Enough of this hypocrisy, Lionel," Adam snapped. "We both know that you're involved."

"I don't know what you're talking about. Apparently I've wasted my time," said Lionel, turning to leave.

"Don't worry, Lionel, your secret is safe with me. I'd just like to chat with you. As you know, your MOD could notify you automatically if this conversation were being recorded," Adam reminded him, freezing Lionel in his steps. "I left my device at home."

Lionel studied Adam for a few tense seconds, then frowned. "I don't have anything to do with this..."

"Your intention was just to stage a robbery," Adam cut

him off. "Putting all the blame on those worthless Chosen… unfortunately Ulysses suffered a heart attack. Who could imagine that on that night your father wasn't in a deep sleep, right?" Adam had Lionel's full attention. "I've been following you for some time, Lionel. I needed to confirm my suspicions: You're the leader of the Raif clan."

"That's been extinct for years!" Lionel shouted back.

"Don't try to fool me…" said Adam, with an ironic smile. "I know enough about your group. My ancestors were former members. I came here to ask you to accept me."

"You must be kidding…" Lionel smiled back.

"Either you accept me as a new member, or I'll have to tell the Council the whole truth," Adam threatened.

Lionel clenched his teeth, then chuckled. "What 'truth,' Adam?"

"You and your clan had the perfect plan to end immigration," said Adam breathlessly. "First you made Victor and George take an Intensifier that had been prohibited, so you could exploit their anger and frustration…"

"Julius did that, not me!" Lionel interrupted.

"Really?" interjected Adam, pausing for effect. "So how come I have pictures of you dropping a red tube."

Lionel's face froze at the sound of Adam's last sentence. "Pictures?" he repeated.

"I don't act without evidence." Adam shrugged. "With

the Intensifiers' help, you made those men confused and enraged, so they went to your father's house to voice their complaints. That's all they wanted – to complain with Ulysses about their lives. Obviously, the Intensifier couldn't force them commit the crime, since it'd be against their true moral principles. But nothing would hold back your plan," Adam concluded, gathering courage to drop his biggest assumption, one that would risk everything. "You relied on your knowledge of acupuncture to resolve the situation, rendering George and Victor unconscious right there in the living-room, with absolutely no memory of how they got there."

Silence. All Adam could hear was the dull roar of the waterfall behind him. He wondered if he had miscalculated... Maybe he had taken things too far.

"Acupuncture?" Lionel burst out in laughter.

Adam knew he couldn't retreat; he needed to give off the appearance of complete confidence. There was still a chance he had guessed correctly. Lionel's hands formed tight fists; he seemed to be incapable of holding back his anger any longer.

"Ulysses wouldn't use anything to protect his documents. He trusted in the inherent goodness of every Gaian, to poison his own papers would've gone against everything he stood for," Adam proclaimed. Something in Lionel's eyes confirmed he was getting warmer. "You didn't want to leave any trace behind, and any chemical means of knocking them out would easily be detected in their blood tests. As a member of the Council you must be an acupuncture expert."

"You've got a great imagination," Lionel replied, but the hesitation in his voice gave Adam more ammunition.

"Everything that you did that day, I practically saw it with my own eyes," he continued, feeling more and more reassured. "I needed to know more about the clan, so I ended up installing a hidden camera in your father's bedroom, a few months ago. It was essential for me to discover more about you."

Lionel started towards Adam, with heavy steps. He stopped just a few inched in front of his face. "You expect me to believe that?" he questioned.

Adam wouldn't be intimidated; instead, he dropped one last bomb. "By the way, did you lose your dragon chain in a fight with your Dad after he saw his own son robbing him... a fight that culminated in his heart attack?"

Lionel grasped Adam by the shirt and seemed to stare straight through him. He cocked his arm back and Adam instinctively closed his eyes, waiting for the punch. But none came.

When Adam opened his eyes, he took a deep breath, relieved. Randy was holding Lionel's clenched fist in the air.

"Adam asked me to attend this *meeting*", said Randy. "I hope you don't mind."

"Thanks, Randy." Adam released himself from Lionel's grip. "I hope you arrived in time to hear it all..."

"I sure did," Randy confirmed, spitting on the ground next to Lionel. "So tell me Lionel... is this all true?"

Lionel met Randy's gaze, not diverting his eyes for a moment or even blinking. Adam was prepared for any flimsy excuse or blatant lie. But not for Lionel's slow, dark smile.

"So he asked you to come here?" Lionel quizzed Randy, his smile widening. "He wanted an ambush?

"Isn't he adorable?" Randy patted Adam on the back, as he and Lionel shared a resonant laugh. "You can save it... Dario's here."

While Adam grasped for answers, the outline of a robust figure took shape in the darkness, as the man clothes' color changed from black to green, like a chameleon. How long had he been hiding there, and why, Adam asked himself. Things weren't adding up, and a wave of panic made it even harder for him to process the situation.

The man drew closer slowly, as though taking pleasure from the distress. Adam racked his brain. "Where do I know you from...?" he asked, recognizing slightly the stocky man, with pale skin, curly hair and big round eyes.

"I'm Dario Walf," the man responded sharply. "I'm the president of the Space Research Center. But I'm also well known for something else..."

Adam had no time to react. It felt like a giant rock had been hurled at his skull, and he collapsed on the ground.

"Nobody punches like Dario!" Randy praised his friend, who smiled with pride, admiring his own fist.

"Adam... Adam Oak..." Lionel grasped Adam's hair and pulled him up to his knees. "How can an idiot like you, who is engaged to a Chosen girl, challenge me?"

"Is he engaged to a Chosen?" asked Dario, loudly. "Randy didn't tell me that!"

Dario dealt Adam another blow, returning him to the ground. Adam dragged himself to his feet, refusing to be humiliated; his nose was bleeding severely and his legs trembled. In response, Dario readied his fist. Adam crouched over in anticipation. Scornful laughter echoed through the clearing.

"How can you be a member of this disgusting clan, Randy?" Adam burst out.

"Don't you dare talk like that about our clan!" Randy retorted, socking him on the jaw. But this time Adam held his place, ignoring his pain, and casting a look of pity out on them.

"You will deeply regret this," Adam snapped. "I left my MOD with a person of trust; it contains the photos of the red Intensifier and images of the crime scene. If I don't return home in two hours, they'll give the device to the new Council president," he said, using up his last bluff. "I'm not stupid."

Instead of giving them pause, Adam's words only provoked them further. His plan had officially backfired.

"Who has your device?" Randy interrogated, grabbing Adam by his hair again and hauling him to the edge of the falls. "Did you give it to your fiancée? I would love to take it from her!"

"She doesn't know anything about it!" Adam shouted. "I'll never tell you where it is!"

"Listen up kid... Lionel just needs a few seconds to erase your memory, like he did with Victor and George," Dario snarled, his face only an inch away from Adam's. "Plus, being the great scientist I am allows me easy access to your memories... It's not going to be a problem discovering who has the pictures."

Dario's words hit Adam harder than his punches had. His panic turned to fear, as he began to process the threat. It would be easy for them to access his memories and call his bluff. They would also figure out that Caroline, Albert, Ruth and Nicolaus were aware of the clan's existence and Lionel's possible involvement in the crime. Of course the clan members would hunt them down and make them suffer before erasing their memories too.

"And we love destroying the Chosen..." continued Lionel. "They're so naïve, they're really the victims of their own weakness..." he smiled grimly. "It was so easy to plant the evidence against Julius... framing him has ended up even better than we'd planned. His conviction will be seen as a huge betrayal to the people who welcomed him, and the Gaians will realize that not a single Chosen is worthy of trust."

"So I guess Randy lied when he said to the press that Julius tried to escape from the IC..." Adam speculated, trying to break free from Randy's grip.

Randy laughed in confirmation, high-fiving Dario. "I was inspired by my friends here.... Dario spiked George's drink like a pro..."

"You're George's boss!" Adam ascertained. "So you're the one responsible for making him explode that day..."

"Yeah, I juiced him up," confirmed Dario, proudly. "Victor was even easier... he accepted my invitation for a drink in the park, while he was walking his dog!"

"Even kids on Earth know you shouldn't talk to strangers!" Lionel taunted.

"Apparently a kid on Earth is smarter than your clan," a voice from behind the trees startled them. Albert stepped forward, arms crossed. "You not only trusted a stranger," he continued, "you even confirmed to him the whole truth about your crimes and the existence of your clan."

"What are you doing here, Albert?" Adam shouted. "I specifically instructed you to stay at home!

"Yeah... I'm not too good at following orders..." responded Albert, diverting his nervousness into irony. When

Adam burst out of Caroline's house, they all knew it had something to do with his speech about friendship and trust. He was going to prove to Albert that he was someone they could rely on. But his desire to help them and his obsession to reveal the truth could put him in real danger.

"I'm definitely not in the mood for a circus night... I don't have the patience to deal with kids..." said Lionel. "Game Over, Adam!" he clapped his hands, addressing him like a child. Lionel pressed his fingers into Adam's neck, making him collapse, unconscious.

"I'm sure you're willing to join Adam on the ground..." said Randy savagely, nearly drooling.

Albert froze. He had never witnessed any real violence and was far from prepared to deal with it. His legs felt weak. Looking towards his friend's lifeless face, Albert wondered if Adam was dead. No, that would only complicate things for the clan. They had just put him to sleep and erase his recent memories. They would still need to access his old memories to find out about the pictures Adam claimed he had taken, and they couldn't do so if he wasn't alive. "No, Randy, thanks," responded Albert, filled with anger. "And by the way, I didn't come here by myself..." he turned and scanned the darkness.

"Let me guess... your sister ran away?" Lionel mocked, approaching Albert. "I don't blame her... now it's your time to say goodnight too!"

"Keep your hands off him," ordered a steady voice.

Lionel and Randy turned to each other, in disbelief, pronouncing the name simultaneously, "Milet?"

"That's right," confirmed the new President, stepping next to Albert. "Glad to see me?"

Albert hoped he had made the right decision bringing Milet along. He didn't have many options anyway. The countdown had begun the moment Adam left, so he had needed to act fast. While Nicolaus and Ruth distracted Caroline, he went to the garage. Yes, he had promised Caroline he wouldn't leave the house, but his intuition was guiding him differently. Before taking the Zoom, Albert had brought up the previously selected destination. After memorizing the name of the park that Adam went, he had headed straight to the Council, where he had managed to catch Milet on his way out. Taken him by the arm and without further explanation, Albert had asked the president to find some Hearing Intensifier and follow him. To Albert's surprise, the president actually went along with it.

"Milet, you know this is just a big misunderstanding, right?" said Lionel, trying to prop up Adam's listless body. But Caroline's fiancée still looked like a broken marionette.

"No, Lionel," replied Milet. "This is a big disappointment. How could you? Since we arrived at this park, we have been listening to your conversation through a Hearing Intensifier. Sadly we heard you attack this young man while we made our way through the forest..." continued Milet. "There's no need to waste our time with your lies, Lionel."

A silence fell over the group, as the plotters scrambled to reorganize their strategy.

"So you listened to our conversation?" questioned Randy, walking slowly towards Milet. "No big deal. You have no proof of what was said today... My MOD would alert me if any other device within miles was recording my voice."

"So what exactly is preventing us from erasing your memories or even throwing your bodies over the edge?" asked Dario, regaining his confidence. "Wouldn't be hard to convince people that you committed suicide..."

Lionel and Randy nodded and moved to flank their guests, who positioned themselves back to back. Albert had never been in a fight and didn't even know if he could deliver a real punch. The only thing he was sure of was that he couldn't run away, even if that meant not getting out alive.

While Randy and Dario headed for Milet, Lionel stalked Albert.

"You're a parasite... you have no value to my society," snapped Lionel.

Albert dodged his first swing. Lionel struck again, but once more punched only the air. The Hearing Intensifier was more useful than Albert had imagined. Like an owl, he used his ears to sense his enemy's next move. The sound of displaced air was enough to give Lionel away. On his third attempt, Albert grabbed a hold of Lionel's arm and delivered a blow with his free hand.

Although his fist felt broken, Lionel barely flinched.

As a response, Lionel kicked his calf, and followed it with a sweep to his legs.

Albert tried to drag himself to his feet, but his knee couldn't stand the weight of his own body. He fell again, and received a kick to the stomach.

Crawling, Albert grabbed a handful of dirt from the ground and threw in Lionel's eyes, making him wince in pain. Enraged, Lionel went for another kick. Albert caught his foot in the air, and spun it with all his strength.

They heard a loud snap and Lionel's scream as he joined him on the ground.

This gave Albert time to glance at Milet to see how he was holding up. To his amazement, Milet was still standing, bruises on his arms and face, while his opponents were lying on the floor with blood flowing from their noses and ears. Apparently, martial arts was another skill on the President's resume.

"Are you okay, son?" Milet turned to Albert.

"Yeah, I'm great," he lied.

Milet reached for his own MOD, and his fingers started sliding through the object.

"Reinforcement?" gasped Albert.

"Better than that... I had an idea..." muttered Milet. "I can't risk having our memories changed before..." he stopped, trying to focus. "I just need a few seconds to set this up…"

"Before we get help? But we need help now!" shouted Albert, foreseeing the next attack. Lionel rose quickly, grasped Albert's hair and, limping, he started to drag his body across the ground towards the edge.

Digging his nails into Lionel's wrist, and agonizing with pain, Albert yelled out to the president for help. But Milet couldn't move. The old man's legs were wobbly, and trembling.

The roar of the falls became louder and louder. It was his time to say goodbye to life, thought Albert, his thoughts drifting to his family. How badly he wished to stay with them that night. How badly he wished to hug them all one last time. Picturing his family together, he stopped resisting.

The pleasant memory numbed his pain as his body fell into the abyss.

Silence. Milet looked in shock to Lionel. The president's mouth opened and closed, but he could not utter a word.

"I'm sure I did him a favor… interrupting such a pathetical little life…" said Lionel, out of breath. "Guess it's your turn now, Mr. President…"

In response, Milet threw his device into the air, where it floated a while, and then expanded, displaying their images on the screen. "Good evening, Gaia!" exclaimed Milet, his eyes wild with panic. "I imagine you are wondering why

I've interrupted your regular programming..." he coughed, trying to retrieve his breath. "Lionel why don't you tell them what we are doing here?"

Lionel hesitated, and then his own device beeped in his pocket, warning that his voice was now being recorded. Milet wasn't bluffing; they were indeed on national television. It was a genius move, but the President hadn't acted fast enough to save Albert.

Lionel turned to address the screen. "I'm sad to inform my fellow Gaians that our president has also turned against us... and unfortunately I haven't gotten here in time to prevent..."

"Don't start with your lies, Lionel!" shouted Milet. "Gaia will know everything that happened here! I will make sure to not forget a single part..."

"It's going to be my word against yours," retorted Lionel. "Who do you think they will believe?"

"They'll have to believe me," another voice interrupted the conversation. Milet's MOD automatically sought out the owner of the voice, and found Albert floating in the air, several feet below the edge.

He felt like hell. The pain was intense, sharp, and multiplied every second he remained upside-down. Not only did his bones feel crushed from Lionel's attack, but now every single muscle felt pinched by a supernatural force. He was alive, though, and wishing he had the strength to kiss his lucky Olympic anklet that he had sworn to never take off until graduation. The metal memento had just saved his life.

"Since I'm not capable of creating fake memories, they will hear exactly what I heard tonight…" shouted Albert confidently to the screen, although his begged for mercy. "So I'd recommend you remain silent and save your performance for the trial," shouted Albert.

For the first time in his life, Lionel followed a Chosen's command.

Sixteen

The day of the trial. The sun was high in the sky, dispelling the clouds that kept trying to cover it. Its reflection on the golden pyramid dazzled Albert's eyes, as he tried to dodge the reporters crowded in front of the Council.

Their brief live transmission a week ago had raised innumerable questions, rumors and speculations. As the key witness, Albert had sworn to keep silent until an official verdict was proclaimed. That meant staying at Caroline's house the whole week, studying and reading. Watching TV had become stressful, as his own face kept showing up on every channel with the most embarrassing nickname he could imagine: *"The Clumsy Chosen Hero"*. Ruth and Nicolaus cracked up every time they found a chance to refer to him that way, like at the dinner table, when asking, "Would the Clumsy Chosen Hero please pass the butter?" At least smiles and laughter had returned to Albert's life.

Like a bodyguard, Caroline tried to protect Albert, Ruth and Nicolaus as they walked towards the Council's entrance. She had gotten pretty mad with Albert and Adam's secret plan – seeing them on television bloodied and bruised didn't help her to excuse their behavior. But after Adam left the hospital fully recovered, except for his missing memories of the night, and Albert detailed the success of their plan, her anger started to melt away.

As they entered the Council, they headed straight towards the chairs reserved for authorized visitors. Isadora glared at them from the row behind, like an eagle about to snatch its prey. Albert met her gaze briefly. The anger buried in his throat threatened to turn into a ferocious verbal attack. But it wasn't worth it. Her red and swollen eyes were proof that she was suffering as much as they had before. He wouldn't waste time beating a dead horse.

"Glad to see you here, Isadora… I remember you saying that Gaia doesn't welcome murderers and thieves… so where are *you* going to live now?" snapped Ruth.

Albert held back a smile. Of course Ruth couldn't pass on such a great line.

Isadora didn't respond, but simply turned to face the opposite direction.

The Council members had already taken their seats and were waiting in silence for the session to begin. Milet's appearance didn't show any sign of recent physical attack. Only his eyes seemed different – grieving and pained. Inside, the wounds were still open, Albert figured.

The suspects entered the room. Albert saw their parents amazed by the presence of Lionel and Randy walking beside them.

Milet rose from his chair, sighed, and diverted his eyes from Lionel's angry stare.

"Good afternoon, everyone. I'm a little short on words today, so I'll let Mrs. Burju Reeh, our new IC chief, do all the talking," said Milet, extending an open palm to the woman seated to his right. Her blue almond-shaped eyes, fine features and familiar last name, convinced Albert that the new IC chief must be Violet's mother.

"I share the same reluctance to talk, as the recent events forced me to reconsider the basic goodness of all Gaians," Burju began, rising from her chair. "Since actions speak louder than words, I'll let you all see the images and sounds extracted from Albert's memories."

The last thing Albert wanted was to hear and to *relive* all those emotions. He was already trying to block out his memories of that night. But it was the only way to show the others exactly what had happened.

The video commenced with Albert and Milet arriving at the park. The sound of their footsteps mixed with Adam and Lionel's argument.

Albert averted his eyes from the screen. Watching a *movie* from his own point of view was just too weird. He turned his attention to those present at the trial. Initially, they seemed lost in the dialogue, but soon the hard and cruel truth hit them violently. Mouths dropped open, eyes became teary, and heads shook in disapproval and disgust. Sarah sobbed. Victor clenched his fists, and Ruth grasped Albert's hand, as though watching a horror movie. Lionel and Randy stared blankly.

When the transmission ended, the members adjourned to a private room to discuss the evidence. A consensus was reached in only a few minutes, and the members returned to announce their verdict.

"First, I want to say that the full video is now being played throughout Gaia," Milet began. "Everybody has the right to know what really happened to our beloved Ulysses and how prejudice can lead us down the wrong path. Unanimously, we declare Victor, George, Sarah, Sophia and Julius innocents of all charges. They were merely victims of a cruel conspiracy." Milet paused to address those he had mentioned. "I couldn't be more ashamed of what happened to all of you. I've always been proud to live in a society that deeply values diversity. That's brought us a richer culture, broader perspectives, and better ways of seeing life. Diversity in Gaia has meant creativity, humor, tolerance and respect for all civilizations. Unfortunately, some people have been busy generating hate for no reason, and for that I apologize."

A council member rose from his chair and clapped his hands slowly. His colleague in the next seat repeated the gesture. Then the whole room joined them.

"Lionel, Randy and Dario we declare you guilty of all charges, conspiracy, discrimination, violence and death threats. For a period of twenty years you will live in a remote place, cut off from all civilization. Daily meditation and hard labor will make up your rehabilitation program."

"I have a daughter to take care of!" shouted Lionel.

"And why didn't you think about her before committing those crimes?" replied Milet. "Your daughter will be under the custody of your only living relative: Julius."

"What? No!" Isadora objected, rising angrily from her chair.

"He's not my relative!" Lionel blustered.

"Yes he is. All allegations that Julius made regarding Ulysses' paternity were verified and confirmed. Ulysses had also confessed the kinship in his will," said Milet.

Perplexed, Lionel turned to Isadora, and mouthed a soundless "I'm sorry."

"It will be an honor for me," said Julius, rising from his chair. "I promise to take care of her as the daughter I've never had."

Without even bothering to disguise her disgust, Isadora shook her head and fled her seat. A guard detained her as she tried to exit the Council.

"I know you'll be a good influence on her, Julius," said Milet. "This trial has now come to an end. Good day to you all."

Albert, Ruth, and Nicolaus sprang into their parents' arms. With a passionate hug, they celebrated their reunion and freedom.

The most poignant moment of the day occurred when they first set foot outside the Council. Hundreds of people were waiting for them, standing in perfect lines. Their white clothes were stamped with the word "SORRY" in dark red ink. Like dominos, they knelt one by one and bowed their heads.

With this symbolic gesture, the Gaians demonstrated humility by fully recognizing their mistakes and sympathizing with the Chosen's pain and sorrow. Nothing else needed to be said.

In the following weeks, Albert, Ruth, Nicolaus and Violet were praised for their investigative work, receiving medals of honor from the Council. Caroline and Adam also gained notoriety, giving interviews on the news and talk shows. Even Soap received gifts from his fans: mountains of chocolate-flavored dog-food.

When things had calmed down, and life seemed to be getting back to normal, Caroline and Adam decided the time had come to celebrate their love and commitment. On a bright night and under a full moon, the couple exchanged vows of fidelity. The party took place on a remote beach, where the waves seemed to have slowed their rhythms to observe the ceremony. Small star-shaped lights were flying above the guests, friends, family members and students.

Albert contemplated the wedding attentively, amazed with how different it was from the weddings he had attended on Earth, and how simple details could have such strong meanings for the Gaians. Starting with the bride and groom's clothes—Caroline couldn't be more beautiful. Two delicate braids united in a high bun, and her long, low-backed dress was radiant yellow, to symbolize happiness. With her bridal gown set against her tanned skin, she seemed to illuminate the night.

Adam's hair was perfectly styled back and a proud smile graced his face. He was wearing a dark blue suit and navy blue shirt. The color was known for representing loyalty and friendship.

The pair's hands were locked together and both were barefoot, standing on a round surface that was floating over the sand and decorated with petals: red roses that symbolized *passion*, and white carnations that meant *pure love*.

Hand in hand, the guests circled the new couple to the sound of a delicate flute. The gesture represented the cycles of life that they would live together, and that had to be dealt with through unity and grace.

When the flute stopped, Caroline and Adam turned to each other and together they pronounced their vows in a loud voice. "I love you and I'll always respect you." There was no priest, no reverend, not even a ring. Their words consecrated their promises and their guests were the witnesses.

Adam tenderly kissed the bride, and addressed the small crowd

"Good evening everyone!" Adam said, with a broad

smile. "First I'd like to thank you all for being here. This is the best day of our lives and I'm glad we could share this with you. Unfortunately, my wife's dad isn't with us anymore, but I've gotta thank him for bringing her here into my life. So, in his honor, I invite you all to dance to his favorite song and tribute to his heritage, a Brazilian classic called 'Eu Sei Que Vou Te Amar' – it means 'I know I'll Love You'…" he said, kissing Caroline one more time.

An instrument that sounded like a cross between a violin and piano began to play; a singer joined them, intoning the beautiful melody.

The circles of guests around the bride and groom slowly dissolved, forming couples that happily danced to the *Bossa Nova* song. While Nicolaus quickly invited a girl to be his partner, Albert remained still, evaluating his situation. He held Ruth's hand on one side and Violet's on the other. The girls seemed hypnotized watching Caroline and Adam dance and whisper to each other. This was the right moment, thought Albert, gathering all his courage to make his move. He let go of Ruth's hand and softly pulled Violet towards him. She silently accepted his invitation to dance, delicately embracing his neck. Violet's sweet perfume disoriented and inspired him at the same time, and he finally spoke his mind.

"You're very beautiful tonight…" Albert began. In fact, he had never seemed Violet so stunning. She was wearing a dark-grey strapless dress, her hair was drawn back and adorned with floral pins. A necklace with one delicate pearl was shining above her chest. A red pearl. The one he had given her. Could that mean something? He hoped it did.

"Thanks, Albert..." said Violet, leaning her chin on his shoulder. "And you're very handsome... your shirt brings out the color of your eyes."

Albert smiled. He had spent several hours trying to choose the right clothes to impress her. At least it seemed that he the time hadn't been spent in vain.

"Your beauty must be rubbing off on me," replied Albert, a little shyly. "I... I think I didn't have the opportunity to really thank you for everything you did for us. You stayed on our side the whole time... without your help we couldn't..."

"That's what friends are for," she cut him off. "You don't need to thank me."

Albert paused. The word *friends* felt like a bucket of cold water. Was that how she saw him? As nothing but friends? Had he been deluding himself all along believing she shared his feelings? He couldn't have misinterpreted her signals... could he? A deep sadness spread over his whole body, and he struggled to keep dancing.

"Violet..." he hesitated. He didn't want his heart crushed that night... he hadn't prepare himself for rejection. But he couldn't bare the uncertainty... the love he felt for her was so intense it was almost suffocating. If she wasn't on the same page, he needed to know... as much as that would hurt. "We're more than just friends though, right?"

"I don't know..." she said, taking a deep breath.

A wave of hope and anguish made Albert's heartbeat accelerate. She hadn't said no. But maybe she was just too polite to hurt him so harshly. Violet straightened up, leaned back off his shoulder, and stopped dancing. He looked down, afraid to face her eyes. That would be easier if she wanted to leave him there... standing alone. But she didn't go anywhere.

"Are we, Albert?" asked Violet, pulling his face up with her long fingers. "Are we more than friends?"

That was the cue he was waiting for. There was no turning back. He grasped both her hands and stared into her eyes. "Would you like to be my girlfriend?"

"That is exactly what I wanted from the moment I first saw you," said Violet, with a smile.

Albert smiled back. He pulled her closer to him, put his arms around her waist and gently kissed her.

Ruth did what she knew she had to do, and disappeared from the scene. After all those months, Albert had finally gathered the courage to express his feelings for Violet, and the last thing Ruth wanted was to spoil their moment.

"Albert and Violet together..." she thought out loud, while walking towards the ocean. That sure would be an interesting thing. Undoubtedly, they were a perfect match and now she wouldn't need to pretend that she didn't realize how madly in love they were. Obviously, she was happy for them, but deep inside she was a little afraid... if anything went wrong with their relationship, she could end up losing her best friend and watching her brother's heart be broken. Well, they probably are soul mates, anyway.

She sat on the sand, letting the waves crash on her feet. She always loved to stare at the ocean. Although its immensity made her feel so small, its beauty and serenity filled her body with hope. Hope for better days, just like this one, with her family and friends together... no worries, no sadness, and no guilt... just joy.

"I was looking for you..." a voice drew her back to the party. "Can I talk to you for a moment?" Phin asked, sitting down right next to her.

"Well, I don't know..." replied Ruth. "I'm a little busy right now..."

"Oh, Ok... sorry..." said Phin, standing up with a jump and quickly turning to leave.

"Hey, come back here! I was just kidding, Phin!" She laughed while grasping his arm. "Of course we can talk."

"Don't mess with me like that," said Phin, sitting again. "I take everything you say very seriously... and by the way, I came here to ask you about that dinner you promised me..."

"I gave you my word," Ruth cut him off, looking towards the ocean. "So I'll accept your invitation."

"I don't want you to feel obligated to accept..." Phin continued, struggling to disguise his nervousness. "I wanna know if you'd *like* to have dinner with me."

"I would love to," assured Ruth, turning to look into his eyes. "Our first dinner was really fun..."

"But I have to tell you that the second dinner won't be about fun..." said Phin.

"No?" asked Ruth, puzzled.

"No. It'll be about being close to you…" replied Phin, with a shy smile. "Still interested in my invitation?"

"Now more than ever," said Ruth, leaning against him as he placed his arm around her shoulder.

Sarah kept her hand on Victor's chest while they danced together. Seeing him smile again brought peace back to her heart. She knew it would take time for the wounds to heal – the false accusations, betrayals and lies. But it seemed that he'd grown wiser in the process. During his time as a prisoner he had dug deep into his own emotions and realized how he had brought pain and division to his family.

Putting his selfishness aside and rearranging his priorities in life, Victor finally saw how much it meant for his family to be living in Gaia. The happiness of his loved ones needed to transcend his own will and whims, and for that, he was making a real effort to fit in.

Sarah waved to Julius. She was so distracted dancing that she hadn't noticed him standing close by. He waved back. It had been a while since they had talked. Since they had been released from the IC, they had only exchanged a few brief congratulations. Before the beginning of the ceremony she had seen him along with George and Sophia. She had a sense that he was making an effort to regain their trust, maybe even start to get their friendship back. Small steps.

"May I interrupt your dance?" Julius asked, approaching the couple. "I'd like to give you this," he continued, extending a small greenish stone. "It's an unpolished stone; a relatively hard rock and a delicate one at the same time, because of its fractures. With dedication and patience, this little thing can be transformed in a shining and beautiful emerald. This stone represents our friendship. I know it doesn't look very nice in the picture right now... but if we smooth it and take care of it..."

"Oh, that was beautiful Julius..." Sarah sighed, looking at the stone placed in the palm of her hand.

"I know that I caused your family a lot of pain. I didn't support you when you needed me most..." Julius paused, reliving his shame. "When Lionel accused me at the Council, I saw how wrong I was. I should have believed in your innocence in the first place and should have fought to prove it. I failed as a friend and I ask your forgiveness."

"You're just as human as everyone else and every human makes mistakes," said Sarah. "I can't imagine how painful it must have been to find out about your father's death."

"I also need to apologize," offered Victor. "I have been quite unpleasant and arrogant, questioning your guidance at every turn... I promise to be on my best behavior from now on. It's my duty... as a friend," he patted Julius on the shoulder. "But I hope you're still willing to be my coach..."

"Of course, that I am, Victor," replied Julius. "I think, basically, I'm demanding more of you because I see your true potential. I'm sure you'll play a big part in the future of Gaia."

"I feel honored by your words, professor. But I hope it's just an opinion.... not a *Revelation*!" he shot back.

Julius laughed along with them. "I guess you'll soon find out."

ABOUT THE AUTHOR

M. Mariz was born in Rio de Janeiro and worked as an actress, lawyer, and writer, with over twenty plays produced. She currently lives in Southern California, where she writes screenplays and novels in Portuguese and English. The Chosen of Gaia was inspired by her own *Revelation* dream.

Made in the USA
Charleston, SC
08 August 2012